Nov. 59

DOCTOR AND SON

'I thought it would be easy settling down as a respectable householder with life insurance and a lawnmower,' writes Richard Gordon's young Dr Simon Sparrow. 'But my wife Nikki and myself found complications. My old friend Dr Grimsdyke made our home a convenient bolt-hole between his own alarming experiences—either as surgeon to a cruise ship filled with irate hypochondriacs, or as resident doctor to a Mayfair hotel, where his unfortunate assessment of a famous actress's condition caused theatrical rather than medical complications. A more disturbing complication was the appearance of my godfather Sir Lancelot Spratt. When he retired from St Swithin's everyone agreed they'd seen the last of the great surgeons; they also agreed that with any luck they wouldn't hear of him again till his memorial service. But Sir Lancelot descended on the home of his mild-mannered colleague Mr Hubert Cambridge to seize control of plans for the St Swithin's Bicentenary celebrations. He also descended on us, and it was unfortunate that his visit suffered such a spectacular curtailment. And there was another complication, too. But he's really what the book's all about.'

By the same author

DOCTOR IN
THE HOUSE

DOCTOR
AT SEA

DOCTOR
AT LARGE

DOCTOR
IN LOVE

THE
CAPTAIN'S TABLE

Doctor and Son

RICHARD GORDON

London
MICHAEL JOSEPH

First published by
MICHAEL JOSEPH LTD
26 *Bloomsbury Street*
*London, W.C.*1
1959

© *copyright 1959 by Richard Gordon Ltd.*

*Set and printed in Great Britain by Tonbridge Printers Ltd, Peach
Hall Works, Tonbridge, Kent, in Baskerville eleven on thirteen point,
on paper made by Henry Bruce at Currie, Midlothian, and bound by
James Burn at Esher, Surrey*

To
KATHARINE

1

'AND how did the honeymoon go?' asked my friend Grimsdyke, as though referring to some popular sporting event.

I winced.

'I wish you wouldn't smirk when you mention it,' I said. 'Even at this distance I'm a bit sensitive about playing the standing joke.'

'Sorry, old lad,' he apologised. 'But you must admit that honeymoons are a bit of a laugh. At least, that's what I thought when I watched you and Nikki going off to a life-time of bliss in a hired Daimler with a couple of tin cans tied to the back.'

'I'll certainly agree with you they're something of an overrated pastime.'

'I bet they are. It must be even worse trying to kid the hotel management you've been married for years and years when you actually *are*. But, bliss apart, did you have a good time?'

I hesitated. 'No,' I said. 'As a matter of fact we ran into difficulties not even envisaged by Havelock Ellis.'

Nikki and I had married unfashionably in the middle of winter, and chose a hotel in Cornwall with blue shutters and pixies on the teapots which seemed to cater only for other honeymoon couples and people convalescing from serious illnesses. We had hardly arrived when my wife started trembling violently. I put this down to emotion, until I discovered that she had a temperature of a hundred and three. So I ordered her to bed and treated her all week for influenza. Then I caught it myself and she had to treat me all the next.

'That wasn't a honeymoon, that was a virologists' convention,' laughed Grimsdyke, as I told him. 'Still, it shows the wisdom of marrying a fellow practitioner. She can not only cherish you in sickness and in health, but cure you free of charge and do your work while you take a gentle convalescence into the bargain. Particularly, of course, when you pick such a good-looking doctor as Nikki. Have another beer?'

We were in the 'Hat and Feathers' at Hampden Cross, a genial inn decorated with sporting trophies chopped from the fore end of deer and the rear end of foxes, which for several centuries had slaked the thirst of the small Hertfordshire town where I practised. We were enjoying the widespread British custom known as 'a quick one before Sunday lunch'—my own wife and others all over the country were sweating over the roast joint and green peas, while their husbands steadily filled themselves with beer until they would as cheerfully have swallowed boiled marbles instead.

I could now seldom visit pubs at all, the doctor's professional reputation suffering from repeated appearances in the local more than the vicar's. But it was the first time I had seen my old classmate from St Swithin's Hospital since he was best man at my wedding. Shortly afterwards

Grimsdyke had found a way of combining his leanings towards both psychiatry and gracious living by becoming resident medical officer to a private mental home installed in a castle in Inverness, and now another winter had passed and spring had arrived with its gift of the English countryside in fresh green wrappings.

'You're not going back to Scotland?' I asked, as Grimsdyke returned from the bar with our tankards.

He shook his head.

'I'm afraid Caledonia's a bit too stern and wild for me. It's wonderful how the inhabitants manage to thrive on draughts and oatcakes. Also, they shut the pubs on Sundays.'

'So you're settling back in London?'

'That's it. The job up north had its uses—particularly in topping up the exchequer, which was pretty low by the time I'd finished paying for your blasted wedding present. But somehow old Uncle Grimsdyke just can't keep away from the bright lights of Piccadilly.'

'There's no one quite so provincial as a Londoner,' I agreed, remembering my own spells of exile, which for a Cockney can be as bitter in Manchester as in Melbourne. The atmosphere of London had by now coloured both Grimsdyke's lungs and personality, and he never felt really comfortable anywhere he couldn't hail a taxi and order it to take him to Fortnum's.

'What's your next contribution to the advance of medicine?' I asked.

He looked rather vague.

'There's my work for the popular press, of course.'

My friend was referring to the knack he had discovered of writing medical articles for the newspapers, which in deference to the strict rules of professional anonymity he generally signed 'By a Distinguished Harley Street Specialist.'

'I've got a rather jolly little thing on deformities coming out on Saturday, by the way, which I'm quite proud of. But first of all,' he went on cheerfully, 'I'm going to have an absolutely slap-up and buckshee holiday. I'm going to be Jolly Jack Grimsdyke. I've got the job as doctor on a Mediterranean cruise ship.'

I was immediately interested. Shortly after qualification I myself had realised that a medical degree is also a ticket to a world tour, and signed-on as doctor to an old cargo boat creaking her way to South America. My professional duties seemed to consist largely of drinking pink gins with the Chief Engineer, and though this was an agreeable form of practice I felt that irreversible psychological changes might occur if I persisted in it.

'That's a bit of luck,' I said admiringly. 'How did you land the job?'

'Through the last one. The chief psychiatrist was treating the daughter of a local laird, a smashing-looking piece who had what he called "a hysterical personality"— though personally I think she only needed her bottom smacked. Still, he must have done her some good, because next week she's marrying young Lord Corrington, who owns the *Lady Anne*—that's the ship, ruddy great white thing like a wedding-cake—and several dozen others besides. Fact is,' he explained, 'the Corringtons are going on the cruise as their honeymoon. She wanted a doctor aboard who knew her case-history, and as the chief psychiatrist couldn't make it he sportingly suggested me. It's just the thing. At the moment I need a rest cure, after more than a year's uninterrupted employment.'

'You might have quite a lot of work to do,' I warned him.

He looked pained. 'Work?'

'I mean, you can't just shut a couple of thousand people up in a tin box and float them into the hot sunshine. They breed infections like mites in Stilton.'

'All that's taken care of anyway,' Grimsdyke said lightly. 'The Chief M.O. is none other than Sir Horace Harberry, M.D., F.R.C.S., and so on, who does it just to pass the time now he's retired. He's a chap who can take out an appendix between lunch and dinner without turning a hair. My duties, I gather, will be of a more social nature—such as showing pretty girls the boat deck in the moonlight. And of course there's bound to be simply hundreds of them on board.'

'All looking for husbands.'

'I think I shall rather enjoy myself,' he went on, ignoring the remark. 'Particularly with refreshments at duty-free prices. How about another pint?'

But I glanced at the clock.

'I promised Nikki faithfully we'd be home by one-thirty.'

Grimsdyke looked surprised. He would not himself have considered leaving until our jovial check-waistcoated landlord, undergoing the twice-daily transformation of an English publican, had hectored us all into the street.

'Come on, old lad! Nikki won't mind, surely? She's a tremendous sport. And everyone knows that pub clocks are kept about twenty minutes fast, anyway.'

'She may be a sport, but I've already discovered there's

no worse crime in the matrimonial calendar than being late for a meal.'

'Oh, all right,' he yielded. 'But it doesn't seem long since there was as much chance of detaching you from an open pub as a thirsty kitten from its mum.'

I had been much looking forward to Grimsdyke's visit, there being few experiences more gratifying to a recently married man than showing off his new wife's cooking to his old friends. He turned out to be a rewarding guest, admiring exuberantly my wife, the roast lamb, the small cottage in which we lived, and even the garden, which was mainly a form of outdoor relief for the birds.

Our conversation during lunch was of the sort inescapable between two Englishmen who'd shared the same educational establishment, and when the time came to clear away Nikki said with some relief, 'I'll leave you two to continue your reminiscences in peace. I can be getting on with the washing-up.'

I gave him a cigar which had originated in the fibrositis of a certain prosperous Major Marston, and he leant back in a thoughtful silence.

'What's it like, old lad?' he asked suddenly.

'What's what like?'

'Well—marriage, and so on. Being a householder with life insurance and a lawnmower. Doesn't the feeling—if you'll forgive my asking—of being rooted to one spot sometimes induce a mild attack of claustrophobia?'

I considered this. I was in practice with a Dr Farquarson, a tall, lean, Scot whom I had met through his being Grimsdyke's uncle. In days when applications for assistantships in general practice pour in as profusely as applications for Wimbledon tickets, I felt lucky to have ended in such a

pleasant spot as Hampden Cross. It was near enough to
London for an occasional night in town, yet far enough
away for an occasional day in the country, and though it
lay huddled in dark conspiracy with fogs most of the
winter even these could be an advantage if the right sort
of people contracted bronchitis.

The letters 'Dr Simon Sparrow, M.B., B.S.' were already
weathering on the name-plate outside our surgery in a
pleasant Georgian terrace facing the Abbey, and after
several years roistering with Grimsdyke round the pubs of
London—an exhaustive knowledge of which seemed the
most substantial remnant of his professional education—I
surprisingly found myself content to spend the evenings
sitting beside the fire trying to finish the crossword.

Grimsdyke's question stimulated me to imagine anything else that I particularly wanted, but I could think
only of a sports car. A doctor spends almost as much time
in his car as he does in his bed, and I was saving up to
drive one of these precarious models along the good old
rambling roads of England. Dr Farquarson was probably
right in declaring this a symptom of persistent immaturity,
but he was a man who held austerely that all cars were the
same as long as they kept the seat of your trousers off the
road.

'Claustrophobia?' I replied. 'No more than lying in a
nice warm bath on a cold and frosty morning.'

'So after a year's sentence, you're still a firm supporter
of the wedded state?'

'I certainly am!'

'I suppose there must be something in it,' Grimsdyke
admitted. 'The last few years all my old chums from St
Swithin's have been mating like mayflies on a hot after-

noon. It's probably one of those things that look more formidable to the onlooker, like eating oysters and ski-ing.'

'Then why don't you try it yourself and find out?'

He looked shocked. 'Don't be silly, old lad. I'm one of Nature's bachelors.'

'Don't let that put you off. The marriage registers are full of them.'

Grimsdyke thoughtfully blew a chain of smoke rings.

'It's an anti-social attitude, I agree. But all sorts of famous chaps have really preferred womanless surroundings—Beethoven, Bluebeard, and so on. Not that I'm anything but an enthusiastic supporter of the fair sex, of course. But in its proper place. Now you've shot into post-graduate status,' he added, giving me an interested look, 'I suppose you must know a hell of a lot about women?'

'Well, I know quite a lot about one.'

'Good Lord, is that the time?' he exclaimed, getting up suddenly. 'I must go and ring the old uncle. It's a bit of a bore, but I simply have to warm the poor old boy's heart by letting him have a look at me from time to time.'

Grimsdyke suffered from the chronic delusion of being Dr Farquarson's favourite relative, though his uncle referred to him at his kindliest as 'that unfortunate mutation in the family breeding pattern.'

'Besides, I want to borrow that big brass telescope he keeps hanging over the fireplace,' he explained. 'Jolly useful for spotting passing ships, seagulls, and so on. That is, if I can convince him first I'm not simply going to pawn it.'

'You can't imagine the delights of a home-made meal to someone who exists largely on a diet of pub sandwiches,' he said a little later, as Nikki and I bade him good-bye at the garden gate. He had announced that he must be off to catch his uncle before the dear old fellow started out for his golf.

'It's always nice to see any of Simon's old friends, Gaston,' said my wife.

He bowed low and kissed her hand.

'And if I may say so, Nikki, you're looking better than ever. Come to that, so does your old man. It must be all that gardening. Personally, it gives me a frightful backache just to walk past Constance Spry's window.'

He started up his 1930 Bentley.

'And now it's Ho! For the open wave,' he called. 'Don't worry, I'll send you a postcard. In a bottle.'

As he roared away to his carefree bachelor life, with nothing more complicated to bother him than where to take his next pint, I realised how much our ways had come to diverge. I felt an involuntary twinge of envy. But it lasted only as long as the reek of his exhaust hung in the mild afternoon air.

2

'SIMON,' said Nikki as we went inside. 'Do you want to go off on a cruise too?'

'Well, you know the old sailor's tale,' I told her gaily. 'Once a man's sailed in a ship's crew, he can't hear a steam whistle again for the rest of his life withou thinking longingly of his suitcase.'

Then to my surprise she burst into tears.

'Nikki, darling!' I exclaimed. I put my arms round her. 'But what on earth's the matter? I was only making a joke.'

'It was—Oh, I don't know.' She dried her eyes briefly with the dishcloth. 'It was the way you watched Grimsdyke drive away, I suppose.'

'Honestly, dearest—it never entered my head. I've swallowed the anchor, as they say. And it's a terribly difficult instrument to disgorge.'

'Simon, dear . . .'

She looked up at me seriously.

'You don't really want to run away and leave me?'

'Leave you? But of course not! What in heaven gave you the idea? Not yet anyway,' I said, as she raised a faint smile. 'Give me a year or two more. Besides, at sea you generally have to wash your own socks.'

'I'm sorry, Simon.' She started to stack away the plates. 'I'm being rather foolish.'

'Now let's not even talk about it any more. Blow your nose and we'll finish the washing-up. Do you know how Grimsdyke does his? He sticks the dishes in the bath and turns on the taps before he goes to bed.'

This incident surprised me. It was so untypical of Nikki, who was a level-headed young woman. She was the product of a medical school not far from St Swithin's, whom I had first met professionally when she came to Hampden Cross to work for me, our roles being rapidly and permanently reversed.

The next few days offered some of the bleak weather which often comes at the end of April to nip an Englishman's sprouting thoughts of deck chairs and cricket fields, and I could prevent myself envying Grimsdyke shortly playing deck-tennis in the Mediterranean sunshine only by imagining him being violently seasick in the Bay of Biscay getting there. He telephoned before he sailed to say that he'd fitted himself out with a naval uniform at a theatrical costumier's, and to ask which was port and which was starboard, explaining that he was leaving the following afternoon from Southampton.

I didn't expect to hear more of him for two or three weeks, but as I snatched my breakfast the morning afterwards I picked up the paper and exclaimed to Nikki in alarm,

'Good Lord, look at this! Grimsdyke's in trouble already.'

There was a small headline on the front page saying DOCTOR TAKEN OFF CRUISE SHIP.

'It isn't him at all,' I added, with some relief.

I read on:

'The luxury liner *Lady Anne* interrupted the start of her annual Mediterranean cruise last night to call at Falmouth and put ashore a sick man. The patient was the ship's own doctor, Sir Horace Harberry, former Harley-street surgeon. Sir Horace told reporters on landing he was not seriously ill. He has a recurrence of an old illness which he cannot risk having treated at sea. The ship sailed later in charge of his assistant, Dr G. Grimsdyke, a London doctor.'

'That's the end of his days in the sunshine,' I said, as Nikki handed back the paper.

'And his nights on the boat deck,' she laughed.

'Poor old Grimsdyke! For the first time in his life he won't be able to shift any patient requiring prolonged mental effort on to the staff of the local hospital.'

My friend's professional predicament was emphasised later that morning by a cable from the *Lady Anne* demanding HOW DO YOU TREAT SPRAINED ANKLE MUMPS LUMBAGO, to which I replied IMMOBILISATION ISOLATION EMBROCATION, and felt rather pleased with myself.

In the next few days I received several more cables from Grimsdyke asking my advice on conditions varying from schizophrenia to scabies, and a scribbled airmail letter from Gibraltar describing his activities in terms which made Florence Nightingale's accounts of the Crimea read like the latest report from the Medical Research Council.

'As long as the lad doesn't kill anyone—and I think he's just about got enough common sense to avoid it—the experience will do him the power of good,' said Dr

Farquarson gruffly. 'For once he can't run away from work, short of turning himself adrift in an open boat.'

'And he was looking on it all as a wonderful cheap holiday,' I said more sympathetically. 'As it is, he'd be far better off if he'd gone to Butlin's.'

I heard nothing more from my friend for a fortnight, when the surgery telephone rang one afternoon and he was speaking himself from Southampton docks.

'Hello, old lad.' He sounded as though he were glancing nervously over his shoulder. 'I'm back on *terra firma*.'

'It's good to hear from you.'

'Can you possibly give me a shakedown for a few days? It's absolutely essential I lose myself in the country for a bit.'

'Of course,' I told him. 'Have a nice trip?'

'Don't be ruddy silly. I've been through something that makes that Kon-Tiki business look like a picnic on the river.'

'Tell me all about it this evening. We'll expect you for dinner.'

'That's very civil of you,' he said gratefully.

'Not a bit. I'm always glad to entertain Jolly Jack ashore. Be sure to bring along your parrot.'

But Grimsdyke only made a rude reply and rang off.

'I don't suppose he'll mind your camp-bed in the sitting-room,' Nikki decided. 'And I'll make a nice curry. I've been meaning to experiment on the recipe for weeks.'

'From his voice on the phone,' I said, 'it might be a good idea to mash in a few tranquillisers.'

I was startled at Grimsdyke's appearance. He had lost

weight, and wore a pale haunted look I had seen before only after his student's *viva voce* examinations with the St Swithin's senior surgeon, Sir Lancelot Spratt.

'Has a ghastly female called Zoë been ringing you up, or prowling round the vicinity?' he asked, almost before we had greeted each other.

'Zoë? Not that I know of.'

'Thank God for that!' He fell into a chair. 'She doesn't know your address, of course, but the beastly woman's got a mind like Sherlock Holmes. Same sort of jaw, too. My flat in Town's completely out of the question, of course. A drink, my dear chap, a drink! I can't possibly tell you more till I've had one.'

'Now you just relax by the fire,' ordered Nikki, as I fetched the brandy bottle from the cupboard it shared with her dust-pans and brushes. 'We mustn't encourage an anxiety neurosis.'

'But what on earth have you done to make this girl pursue you?' I asked, pouring him a stiff dose.

'You might as well ask the same question of some poor innocent lamb being pursued by a tigress.'

'Tell us about it when you've had some food,' said Nikki. 'The curry will be ready in a minute.'

'Curry!' exclaimed Grimsdyke, so violently that I thought he was going to be sick on our hearthrug.

'But don't you like curry?' I asked. 'When we shared digs you used to be rather fond of it.'

'And so I was. But many things in my life have changed these last two weeks. Curry, let me tell you, was served for every meal on board the *Lady Anne*, including breakfast. By now I feel like a fire-eater in need of a holiday.'

'Of course, she usually sails to the Far East,' I re-called.

'Yes, the beastly ship's still all pukka sahib and punka wallah, and you half expect General Gordon to come strolling out of the Veranda Café. The whole crew looked on cruising as terribly *infra dig*, like having to open up the old stately home to the public.'

Calming down a little and remembering his usual good manners, Grimsdyke then assured Nikki that he would enjoy his curry to the last mouthful.

'By now, of course,' he said, as we sat round the table, 'I never want to see a ruddy ship again, even the Woolwich Ferry. But I don't mind telling you that when I stepped aboard the *Lady Anne* at Southampton docks I was as blithe as young Jim Hawkins. The thing seemed as high as the white cliffs of Dover, and looked very comfy. I was shown to a cabin somewhere below the engine-room, but that didn't worry me. And I then reported smartly to Sir Horace Harberry.

'I'd somehow imagined Sir Horace to be a jovial Captain Cuttle sort of chap. But he's a tall pale fellow with a wing collar who looks as though he's been brought up on a diet of birdseed. Also, he has no sense of humour. I tried a little light conversation, but he just said something about having one of his attacks of indigestion and packed me off to see the Captain.

'The Captain, at least, I expected to be a merry old sea-dog—look at the pictures you see in the advertisements, with children crawling all over them on the bridge. But this one was a haggard fellow with bushy sidewhiskers who reminded you of those portraits of the Duke of Wellington. And he didn't have any sense of humour, either. To break

the ice, I made a few light-hearted remarks about it being
very jolly for him having a wife in every port, but he didn't
seem to catch on. He just said, "Doctor, have you been in
ships before?"

'And I said, "Of course."

'And he said, "Which ones?"

'And I said, "The ones that go from Dover to Calais
and back."

'There was a bit of a silence then. He just shook his
head rather slowly and handed me a copy of *Regulations
for Ship Surgeons*, a thing about the size of the family
Bible.

' "You will particularly remember, Doctor," the Captain
went on, "that your bar account is strictly limited to
fifteen shillings weekly, and that you are not allowed to
cultivate the friendship of any particular passenger. Also
that you may converse with female passengers on deck
after nightfall only when it is essential for the safety of the
ship. Good afternoon." '

Grimsdyke took another gulp of brandy.

'So for a start it didn't look as if I'd be able to get some
nice girl alone between the lifeboats unless the ruddy thing
was actually sinking. However, I didn't have much time to
brood about this, because the passengers were now coming
aboard. So I went on deck and hung over the rail to see
what my future shipmates would look like.'

'All the nice girls, you mean?' asked Nikki.

Grimsdyke snorted.

'Nice girls! You might as well have looked for nice girls
coming up the gangway of the Ark. Of course,' he added
bitterly, 'if I'd any sense I'd have realised before I let
myself in for the trip that—despite all those fraudulent

pictures in the travel agents'—no-one under sixty could possibly afford a ticket on a tub like that. The entire passenger list now came tottering up looking as if they'd been advised by their doctors to take a long sea voyage for their health. That's rubbish to start with,' he added warmly. 'Believe me, you've got to be absolutely fighting fit to face a Mediterranean cruise.'

'I think the advice to take a voyage is generally given to old chronics, to get a holiday for the doctor who's fed up with the sight of their faces,' I suggested.

'Damned unprofessional conduct, if you ask me,' muttered Grimsdyke.

He hesitated, then pushed his plate aside.

'Do you think I could just have a little cheese?' he said weakly.

'Perhaps you're right,' said Nikki. 'I rather suspected one of the eggs was a bit off, but it was masked by the Bombay Duck.'

'It seems very tasty to me,' I told her dutifully. Nikki was as anxious as any other new wife to woo her husband's stomach, but our menus sometimes suffered from her insistence that cooking was only a branch of biochemistry. 'And anyway, to-day I didn't get any lunch. Go on, Grim.'

'There was a great deal of bustle and several old boys called out to me, "Steward! Fetch me a large whisky-and-soda!"' Grimsdyke continued. 'But at last we made for the open sea. Then we'd hardly got past the Isle of Wight when old Harberry summoned me. At first I thought he'd relented and asked me down to his cabin for a gin. But instead he gave me a sort of clinical *viva*.

' "How would you treat single-handed a well-preserved

elderly gentleman who'd perforated his duodenal ulcer?"
he asked me.

'I thought for a moment and said, "Open him up and
sew up the hole."

' "You have, young man, a considerable experience of
this operation?" he went on.

'I hedged a bit, and then I said there had to be a first
time for everything.

' "Explain to me, then, precisely how you would set
about it?" '

'So I told him—to the best of my knowledge. Then he
gave a groan and disappeared into his bathroom. The next
thing I knew he was going over the side with his suitcase
and leaving the lot to me.'

'A bit of a blow,' I agreed.

'A blow, but not a knock-out. The Grimsdykes, old lad,
have their faults, but they always rise to the occasion when
they're absolutely forced to. Refusing to be daunted, I
found a very useful little book tucked away called the *Ship
Captain's Medical Guide*, which explains how to tackle pretty
well everything from broken legs to bedbugs in hearty
language that sailors can understand. And with the aid of
your invaluable cables I settled down to cope.'

'But surely there must have been someone on board to
help you?' asked Nikki.

'Oh, yes. Two nursing sisters who seemed to have been
recruited from the sick bays of military prisons, and a
hospital orderly who drank all the surgical spirit.'

'So you didn't have much time for the social life?' I
remarked.

'My professional trials,' Grimsdyke went on sombrely,
'were nothing—absolutely nothing—to what I had to put

up with on the social side. As a matter of fact, I can hardly
bring myself to think of it.'

'Have some more brandy,' I said.

'And let's sit round the fire,' said Nikki. 'It's much more
appropriate for telling tales of adventure at sea.'

3

'I HAD my own table in the dining saloon,' Grimsdyke went on, when we had rearranged ourselves. 'I played host to five passengers. I can see them now.' He stared round glassily. 'Mr and Mrs Slingsby, the Reverend Peckhorn, Miss Hales—ghastly woman, all beads and spiritualism—and Major Dampier.

'For some reason the ship's Purser, who incidentally had the only nice-looking bits on board sitting at his own table, seemed to imagine that doctors enjoy talking only to interesting invalids. And this lot were certainly interesting —to themselves. They had enough wrong with them to restock the pathology museum in the Royal College of Surgeons.

' "Doctor," Miss Hales would begin, just as I was tucking into my plate of curry. "I'm sure you'll be most interested to hear about my kidney. Just a bag of stones, that's what the doctors called it. Why, I'm lucky to be here at all."

'She would then give a textbook account of her nephrectomy, ending up of course by claiming that her kidney was quite the worst the surgeon had ever laid hands on. Odd, isn't it, that people wouldn't dream of boasting in public about their bank accounts or front gardens, but when it comes to their illnesses there's no holding them?

'Of course, Mrs Slingsby immediately took up the challenge and weighed in with her goitre, which they'd invited surgeons from all over London to see taken out, and Major Dampier followed up smartly with his prostate and the Reverend Peckhorn with his jejunal diverticulum. I didn't mind giving these organs my best and keenest attention at the right place and time,' Grimsdyke concluded warmly. 'But it was about the end having them served with all my meals.'

I felt this was the moment to pour him another brandy.

He sat for some moments staring into the fire in silence, until Nikki asked gently, 'How about Zoë?'

He gave a brief sigh.

'I told you there were a few girls on board, didn't I? Well, Zoë was one of them.'

'Was she nice?' I asked.

'She was about six feet tall,' he said, 'and she shook hands like a pair of nutcrackers. She was also a born organiser. At home I bet she captains the tennis club and runs all the fêtes. On board she organised the Sports Committee, of which I found myself an *ex officio* member. There were about six of us, who met every morning in the Veranda Café, to arrange all those silly games people wouldn't dare to be seen playing on dry land. That was fair enough. But pretty soon she was organising me.

'The main trouble with a ship,' he went on, taking another drink, 'is that you can't get away from people, except by chucking yourself over the rail—which I considered more than once. Everywhere I went, Zoë was sure to go. I've never met a woman with such a capacity for being round the next corner. And every time she greeted me with something like, "Haven't you played your shuffleboard heat with Mr Carter-Berrison yet, you naughty boy? He's been waiting half an hour and getting ever so shirty." Nauseating, you'll agree? Worse than that, she entered me for every damn contest going, from chess to high-diving. That was a terrible shock to a man whose daily exercise has for years been confined to winding up his wrist-watch before going to bed.

'But worse disaster was in store. For some reason she took a tremendous fancy to me. God knows why. But you know how girls think doctors are wonderful? Particularly when they're all decorated with gold braid and brass buttons. Rumours got round the ship. People began to giggle and give us significant glances over their morning cups of beef tea. Then one afternoon,' he went on, his voice starting to shake, 'when we were all alone in the games room and had just finished our ping-pong heat, she kissed me. I shall never forget it. It was like being run over by a tractor. After that I had to slink about the ship like a ruddy stowaway. Then the horrible woman wormed my address out of the Purser, and is probably at this very moment squatting on my doormat with an invitation for mixed hockey next Sunday.'

'A soul-testing experience,' I observed feelingly.

'But a mere nothing,' he continued with masochistic pride. 'To my real trouble aboard.'

'Surely there couldn't be anything worse than Zoë?' asked Nikki.

'There was. In the person of her ladyship, my prime patient.'

'The only reason you were there at all,' I reminded him.

'Knowing her psychological history, I suppose I should have been prepared for the worst when she came up the gangway, with her new husband and enough luggage for a touring pantomime. It soon turned out that she was one of those unfortunate people who vomit almost as soon as they see a sign with the words "Boat Train." '

'What a bit of bad luck, Grim,' I sympathised. 'They couldn't even cure Lord Nelson of that.'

'Lady Corrington started being seasick as soon as we got into the Channel. I treated her with antihistamines and hyoscine and so on, of course. But I might just as well have given her aniseed balls. Therapy was further complicated by Lord Corrington, who not only regarded her as a fragment of Dresden china but was a pretty nasty piece of work himself into the bargain.

' "Can't you cure a simple case of seasickness, Doctor?" he used to bark at me every time I appeared in their cabin. "I should have thought the merest medical student would have known the remedy for that. Thank God I go to an osteopath!" '

'Did you try all the traditional cures?' I asked.

'Oh, the lot—a raw egg in Guinness, bandaging one eye, cold compresses on the umbilicus. Eventually I decided that only psychiatric treatment would do. But like a chump I told his Lordship first that his wife was inclined to be somewhat hysterical, and that did it. He took this as a tremendous insult not only to his family, but to the entire British aristocracy.

'There was quite a scene. He said something pompous about breeding, though everyone knows his old man only got a peerage by swindling the Government all the way through the last war. He stopped short of actually challenging me to pistols at dawn on the boat-deck, but he made nasty remarks to the Captain, who henceforward looked at me like the Duke of Wellington with his mind on Napoleon. It hurt my professional pride, old lad, apart from everything else. I redoubled my therapeutic efforts. I tried hypnosis. I told her to think about the Sahara Desert. But to no avail.'

'Did you consider half a bottle of dry champagne?' I suggested.

'Of course I did. Just a terrible waste of good champagne. Every morning, regular as clockwork, the damn woman would be seasick. Why, even as we were sailing up Southampton Water to-day she lost her breakfast. It was just—what's the matter, old lad?'

I burst into a roar of laughter.

'Personally, I can't see anything funny in it,' he said, as Nikki joined in.

'My dear chap! You really are an idiot. Why didn't you think of asking her——'

'I don't find anything hilarious about the case at all.' He sat looking like a man whose friends have just sportively set alight his newspaper. 'She was an extremely trying clinical problem——'

'But surely you remember what the rude obstetricians taught us at St Swithin's? Always suspect the condition first in any female outside a nursery or a nunnery.'

'I don't follow you,' he told me haughtily. 'If you imagine you know the cause of seasickness——'

'I certainly know the cause of this seasickness. In a few months' time it'll be pushed along in a pram.'

'But that's impossible!' Grimsdyke exploded. 'They'd only been married a couple of days.'

'Grim, old man, really! After all these years of professionally studying human nature——'

'Good God!' He stared wildly into the fire. 'Now you come to think of it—— But damn it! I must say, it was ruddy unreasonable of the blasted woman.'

'Any female between the age of nine and ninety——,' I quoted, as Nikki and I continued to laugh at his expense.

'Well, I bet you wouldn't have spotted it yourself in the circumstances,' he muttered crossly. 'But I'd like to have a look at his Lordship's face when he finds out,' he added, cheering up a little. 'I knew he was just the sort of chap who'd cheat under starter's orders. Anyone could tell that the fellow wasn't a gentleman.'

The conversation flagged after that, and shortly Grimsdyke abruptly announced that he was tired and wanted to go to bed.

'Poor old Grim,' I said to Nikki, when we left him on my ramshackle camp-bed in the sitting-room. 'I only hope the story never gets to the ears of Sir Lancelot Spratt.'

'These things could happen to anyone,' observed Nikki charitably.

'Oh, I agree. But they only do seem to happen to Grimsdyke.'

It may have been Nikki's curry, or it may have been punishment from my subconscious for mocking my friend, but that night I dreamt that I was a doctor on a vessel the cross between the *Flying Dutchman* and the *Queen Elizabeth*, with everyone aboard being sick in the teeth of a violent gale. And when I was woken by Nikki stirring beside me at daybreak, I felt definitely queasy myself.

'I've just been sick,' Nikki announced.

'It must have been that curry,' I said sleepily. 'I'll go and get you some bicarb.'

I had to disturb Grimsdyke as I picked my way to our domestic drug cupboard in the corner of the sitting-room, but he only grunted and went to sleep again. When I got back to the bedroom I was surprised to find the light on and Nikki sitting up in bed looking pleased with herself.

'Here's your soda bic.,' I said, stirring the mixture. 'I've made it strong enough to neutralise even Bombay duck.'

'Darling,' said Nikki. 'Kiss me.'

'Kiss you?' I looked surprised. 'But a moment ago I thought you were at death's door?'

'You know, you wouldn't have been any cleverer than Grimsdyke,' she said, holding out her arms.

'Good God!' I dropped the glass. 'Do you mean you're——?'

'Of course I am, my sweet. That's why I became so weepy and emotional the other day when I thought you wanted to run away from me and go off to sea. Pure female hormones.'

'Nikki darling!' I cried, hugging her. 'This is absolutely wonderful! It's terrific!'

'It's only natural.'

'But for God's sake,' I added quickly. 'Not a word to Grimsdyke.'

'Of course not,' she said. 'And do you know, it's a funny thing but there's nothing I want more in the world at the moment than avocado pears stuffed with tinned sardines.'

4

I HAD already had forty-two babies, all fathered on me by the Medical Acts and dedicating their first few minutes of life to teaching me the elements of practical midwifery. They had been born either in the highly organised atmosphere of the St Swithin's Maternity Department, or in the highly unorganised one of the dwellings huddled round the hospital walls and known for this purpose as 'The District.' But wherever the event took place, it always scared me greatly. Fumbling my way with sheets of newspaper and saucepans of boiling water in small insanitary bedrooms, my professional attention often distracted through the seat of my trousers being roasted by the traditional roaring fire, I could only repeatedly congratulate Nature on evolving a practically foolproof process.

But having a baby myself came as something of a shock. I suppose it does to any young man, despite the strong words of the marriage service, which he is probably at the time too distraught to hear. I also felt tremendously proud of myself. On reflection, this seemed remarkably stupid for achieving something within the reach of every zoological

B   33

organism more advanced than the protozoal pond-dwellers, who reproduce themselves simply by splitting in two down the middle.

I was wholly unable to keep the good news to myself, and the following morning when Nikki rose from the breakfast table and made for the bathroom with the businesslike step of all such cases, I explained rather coyly to Grimsdyke that she was 'suffering from a touch of the pregnancy.'

'Good God, old lad!' He stared at me as if I had just announced my intention of taking Holy Orders. 'What, you mean——? How long has this been going on?'

'So shortly it's almost indecent to mention it.'

'Old Simon Sparrow to be a daddy,' he murmured unbelievingly. 'It shatters me a bit. Particularly when I recall our jolly days as students at St Swithin's. It's quite a strain seeing you patting the young chap on the head and handing him half-a-crown with a stern warning not to spend it on drink.'

'That scene's a long way ahead yet, anyway. And don't forget it's an even chance it'll turn out female.'

'And ninety to one it's twins,' said Grimsdyke, who had a head for such things. 'I suppose I shouldn't really be surprised. Look at old Tony Benskin—he was one of the lads in our youth and no mistake, and now he's got hundreds of them. Anyway, hearty congratulations to you both, and I hope I'll be invited to take a glass of champagne at the christening. I must say, after my experiences in the beastly boat there does seem to be a lot of that complaint about at this time of the year.'

Dr Farquarson, my partner, was unimpressed—but after a lifetime of practice all over the world he would have been unimpressed even by witnessing the birth of Aphrodite.

'I suppose your good lady's perfectly certain of her diagnosis?' he asked. He never smiled, but his eyebrows quivered when anything struck him as particularly amusing. 'I've always held that lady doctors were never much good at that particular subject.'

I looked alarmed. 'Good Lord, I hadn't thought of that.'

'Now, that half-witted nephew of mine would improve immeasurably if he'd only settle down and found a family,' he went on, scraping out his pipe with an old scalpel lying on his consulting desk. 'Preferably under the thumb of some strong-minded woman. He looked in while you were out on your rounds, by the by, with some ingenious story of dropping my telescope overboard. I rather expected I'd seen the last of it when I lent it to him. He also tried to give the impression that he'd suffered the worst nautical hardships since Captain Bligh was set adrift from the *Bounty*.'

'He really did have a bad time of it,' I told him, in defence of my friend. 'Anyway, before he can start a family he'll have to start a job. And believe me, Farquy, he's been seriously discussing plans with me for several jobs the last couple of days.'

'He has with me, too. He's heard somewhere the World Health Organisation are looking for a doctor to prepare a report on the loose women of South America, and he seems to think he's their man. I hope he finds employment of some sort soon, if only for your sake. Otherwise he'll be battening on you until it's time for your child to go to school.'

The same day I proudly telephoned the news to my

father, a busy G.P. on the south coast. But the announcement was complicated through his taking the call in the middle of his evening surgery.

'Boil up plenty of water and keep your wife warm and I'll be round in a couple of shakes,' he said at once. 'Is she having nice pains? One moment—no, no, Mrs Hartridge. It's the smelly stuff in the big bottle you rub on your leg, and the white mixture in the little one you swallow. No wonder your arthritis hasn't been getting any better. Hello? Hello? Don't worry my dear fellow, everything's going to be absolutely all right. Perfectly natural process, remember. Just get the cot and all the etceteras ready and tell her not to bear down till I arrive.'

The revelation to my wife's parents was less clinical, Nikki dropping the information in a well engineered casual remark over tea the next week-end. This immediately swept the conversation with a flurry of technicalities about the coming baby's equipment, which seemed to me more complicated than a jet pilot's.

'And when are you going to have him, my darling?' asked her mother, making a sweeping embryological assumption.

Nikki laughed. 'Oh, not for ages and ages. According to the book, next New Year's Day at the earliest. And at the moment I can hardly believe I'm going to have one at all.'

'It goes like a flash,' said her mother, though sounding disappointed that we couldn't produce the following week.

'What's all the fuss about?' asked my brother-in-law, a pink-faced young man in twill trousers.

'It's just that about next Christmas your sister will be retiring from the world,' I told him, feeling a little shy about it.

'Retiring? But whatever for?'

'She's breeding.'

He seemed puzzled. 'Breeding? Breeding what?'

'Well, not Sealyhams. We're having a baby.'

'Good God, are you really? What, old Nikki with a baby? You don't really mean it, do you? I've never thought of her doing anything like that at all. Mind you,' he went on, recovering himself, 'if you'd waited a bit and had it just before the fifth of April, you'd have got a whole year's income tax rebate. All the smart chaps I know in the City do. Congratulations, of course.'

But I got the impression that he took it all as a personal insult.

'It seems silly that I can't make any further contribution to the process except holding the wool for the bootees,' I remarked to Nikki as we drove home. 'I suppose I must take comfort from the male codfish, which I believe fertilises a million eggs in an afternoon and swims away into oblivion.'

'You'll have quite enough to do later on, dear,' she said. After a pause she added, 'This baby's going to make quite a lot of difference to our lives.'

'A pretty understatement.'

'And it's going to make quite a lot of difference to me.' She looked fondly at her feet. 'I can hardly imagine myself as one of those captive balloons we see sailing round the antenatal clinic.' Nikki hesitated. 'You won't hate me then, Simon, will you?'

'Hate you?' I said in surprise. 'But whatever for?'

'It's a form of the subconscious guilt-complex. Didn't you know? It's what the psychiatrists say.'

'If we believed all the psychiatrists say we'd never get

around to having any children at all,' I told her. 'I promise I'll be the model expectant father—always at your side, giving moral support and helping with the washing-up to the end.'

Such resolutions were easier because Grimsdyke, perhaps deciding that he would be *de trop* at such a delicate time or perhaps preferring to face Zoë than another night on my camp-bed, had returned to the small flat he rented in Chelsea. I settled down to adjust myself to the psychological demands of incipient fatherhood for some quiet weeks, until he communicated with us again. The telephone rang one evening, and I was less surprised to hear from him than the number from which he was calling.

'Hal—oo?' said a finishing-school voice on the end of the line. 'Dr Spar—oo? This is the Arundel Hotel, London. I have Dr Grimsdyke for you. One moo-ment, please.'

'It's Grimsdyke, from the Arundel,' I whispered to Nikki across the sitting-room.

'What on earth's he doing in an expensive place like that?' she asked, with a frown.

'I expect he's found some way of phoning free of charge from the gents'.'

But Grimsdyke's voice came on the wire saying, 'Ah, thank you, Miss Sherrington. Hello? Hello, old lad. Can you come and have a drink with me some time pretty soon?'

'I'm practising hard to play the stern parent,' I told him. 'But I'm still ready to have a drink with you at any time. Where do you suggest?'

'Here, of course.' He sounded rather hurt. 'This is not only to issue an invitation but to inform you of change of residence. Henceforward I am to be found at Suite 12a,

The Arundel Hotel, Mayfair. Jolly sight more comfortable than your camp-bed, too.'

'My dear chap, do be careful!' I exclaimed. 'You can get into the most frightful trouble in the courts these days, flitting about and not paying hotel bills.'

'What an unworthy suggestion! Surely you don't imagine I'd do anything like that? Anyway, I won't have a chance to, because there isn't going to be any bill. I'm on the staff—resident physician to the Arundel, no less. Just the job. You don't have to shake your thermometer down, you dip it into the nearest champagne bucket. When can you come and help me to get through my entertainment allowance?'

We arranged to meet the following Thursday evening, when I should be in London for my weekly part-time (and unpaid) work at the St Swithin's Hospital gastric clinic.

'I must say, Grimsdyke's new job would give me a frightful inferiority complex myself,' I said to Nikki, recounting our conversation. 'But it sounds like the one he's been looking for ever since I've known him. For once he'll be able to live above his income without it mattering.'

'I'm quite sure he's made a terrible mistake,' Nikki disagreed. 'He's reached the age when he ought to settle down to a steady job with a future, instead of eternally flitting about like some sort of medical moth.'

'Well, you know old Grim,' I told her resignedly. 'He'll never be the staid practitioner dishing out weighty advice across the top of his finger-tips—he doesn't take himself half seriously enough. Besides, you only see doctors like that in the malted milk advertisements. Yes, it'll be fun to have a comfortable drink in a really first-rate London hotel,' I went on in pleasant anticipation. 'Even at the

annual hospital ball we used to whisk the girls out to the
nearest pub between dances to cut down on expenses.'

I was thinking again about Grimsdyke's professional
career as I drove my small saloon car through the rush-
hour traffic in Piccadilly the next Thursday. I supposed
that he was really too much of an individualist to be a
successful family practitioner. Doctors differ, but even in
medical school they start conforming to type—all the
hearty students at St Swithin's who went mountain-
climbing and beer-drinking seemed to take up surgery, the
quiet ones covered with spots and the dust of the library
shelves turned into successful physicians, the gloomy men
who smoked dirty pipes and spat in the laboratory sinks
were later pathologists, and all the mad ones, of course,
became psychiatrists. But Grimsdyke was more enterprising and extroverted than any of us, and would probably
have fitted satisfactorily into the national medical structure
only as the Minister of Health.

I found him waiting inside the revolving doors, dressed
like a successful young barrister.

'Jolly nice to see you, old lad,' he greeted me warmly, as
a man like a City toastmaster stripped off my coat. 'Where
would you like to go for a drink?'

'In the bar, I suppose,' I said, looking round with some
reverence.

'We have five cocktail bars here,' he explained proudly.
'What do you think of my new home?'

The Arundel seemed probably the most exclusive, and
certainly the most expensive, hotel in the West End. It had
none of the *Palais de Versailles* air of big hotels all over the
world, but was one of those smaller ones in London which
are decorated to provide an intensely English atmosphere.

The hall contained an open fireplace wide enough to spit an ox, flanked with suits of armour so well burnished they looked ready to go out and give battle in Berkeley Square. Beyond them an Adam staircase cascaded to the feet of a marble nude, whose attitude and bust measurement were more modest than some of the women I noticed sitting about in the lounge. The place seemed intended to give guests the impression of staying in the country seat of some fine old English nobleman; and it was full of Americans, who were the only people who could afford to stay there.

'Very charming,' I said.

'The American Bar will be nice and empty,' suggested Grimsdyke. 'It's the only place the Americans don't seem to go. And don't worry about the drinks,' he added, as I followed him through another luxurious lobby. 'I just sign for them. A very convenient arrangement, don't you think?'

'But how on earth did you manage to get a magnificent job like this?' I asked, as we sat down in a corner of the bar.

'The Grimsdykes, old lad, may often be on their uppers,' he explained a little grandly. 'But they always fall on their feet. Do you remember Miss Hales?'

I frowned.

'Which one of your girl friends was that?'

'No girl friend. Miss Hales was at my table on the ship. She was the one with the kidneys, which she talked about every time she could get them in edgeways. Fortunately for me, as a conscientious servant of the shipping company I lent a sympathetic ear, instead of shoving her through the nearest porthole in the public interest. It was only when presenting my modest account at the end of the voyage that I discovered she lives here permanently. When she volunteered that the dear hotel doctor had been carted off to hospital—with symptoms sounding to me suspiciously like cirrhosis of the liver—I smelt the chance of a job. She very decently said she'd have a word with the management, and I can only suppose the old bird runs up a fantastic bill here every week, because they just told me to come along.'

'And very nice, too.'

He paused.

'Yes and no. Mind you, this is the way I really like to live—*cordon bleu* cuisine, early tea and biscuits in bed, chap to press your pants, and within a taxi-hoot of Piccadilly Circus. The snag is, they give me a reproduction of Nell Gwynn's bedroom and plenty to eat and drink, and damn all else. Why, it'll take me months even to pay for these togs I had to buy.'

'But surely you've got lots of rich and aristocratic patients?' I asked in surprise.

'Indeed,' he agreed, 'I have what you might call an *embarras de duchesse*. But the blasted manager only lets me keep ten per cent of the fees. You can't imagine what a mean bunch they are backstage,' he went on indignantly. 'If I ran a place like this, you'd see me on the doorstep day and night welcoming my old friends to wine and dine lavishly at my expense. But this lot pretty well count the bubbles in the soda-water. However, I didn't ask you here to weary you with the trials of a hotel doctor's life. Fact is, old lad, I want a bit of professional advice. And at this particular moment you seem just the man to give it to me.'

'I don't suppose I can be of much help,' I said, wondering what trouble he had got himself into now. 'But I'm more than ready to do my best.'

'Let's have another gin,' said Grimsdyke, reaching for his pencil. 'And I'll tell you all about it.'

5

WHEN the waiter had served our drinks as though presenting a humble petition to royalty, Grimsdyke looked over his shoulder, lowered his voice, and asked:

'Have you heard of Monica Fairchild?'

'What, the actress? Of course I have.'

'She lives here, too. Damn great suite on the top floor, like the National Gallery. With an entourage consisting at the moment of one husband and one secretary.'

'And she's one of your patients?' I said, looking at him with greater respect.

He nodded.

'I'd better start by explaining that she's a rather difficult one. In fact, I'll go so far as to say that I've met some pretty difficult women in my time, but I'd rather face Boadicea in her chariot any day.'

He broke off as a thin man in rimless glasses glanced into the bar.

'Good evening, Mr McGlew,' said Grimsdyke politely. 'And how is the oesophagheal dysfunction this evening?'

'O.K., Doc.,' grunted the man. 'Just looking for the wife.'

'That's Mr Harry McGlew,' Grimsdyke explained, as he withdrew. 'He made fifty million dollars from canned pork and has to live on boiled fish. Serves him right, if you've ever tasted the stuff. Did you notice the technical terms, by the way? Very keen on them, the Americans. I have a hell of a job keeping one disease ahead of the patients, though reading up the medical section of *Time* helps no end. But I digress.

'I first made the acquaintance of Miss Fairchild,' he continued, 'at two o'clock in the morning, when I was summoned by the young woman who's her secretary with the news that the great actress was dying. And when I reached the bedside I damn well thought she was. She looked absolutely on her last legs, and was crying hoarsely for people to summon her mother and her agent. Then I took another look, found temperature and pulse were all right, and after puzzling it out a bit I suddenly remembered that she's currently playing Desdemona at the Old Vic, much to the appreciation of press and public. Do you see the point, old lad? It was all part of the act.

'I think all actresses are a bit potty,' Grimsdyke declared warmly. 'And I've known a few of them in my time. Not in the Fairchild class, of course—most of mine were eking it out with a bit of chorus work in the provinces. Now, I don't really believe Miss Fairchild was creating for the hell of it. She just felt like death, as most of us do from time to time, and thought that was the way you went about it. Actually, she was constipated.'

'At least, she's an interesting patient,' I murmured consolingly.

'Again, yes and no. The Fairchild is not only a shocking hypochondriac, but she's somewhat imperious. I suppose when a thousand or so people clap you to the echo night in and night out you begin to get the inkling you're some-one pretty damn important. As soon as she discovered that she wasn't in fact dying, she demanded, "Who is this mere boy at my bedside? Bring me a proper physician." Annoyed me a bit at first, until I realised that it was really Lady Macbeth speaking. After that we got on rather better. She even took a fancy to me, in a distant sort of way. The only snag came when I wanted to examine her. Wouldn't let me inspect her chest at any price. If I want to have a look at her sternal region, it seems I'll have to wait until she's in Restoration comedy.'

At that moment we were again interrupted, by the appearance of a rather plain girl of about nineteen with pony-tail hair, tartan trews, and upswept glasses and an upswept bosom.

'Ah, there you are, Dr Grimsdyke. I have a message for you.' Her voice dropped reverently. 'From Miss Fairchild. She wishes to see you when she returns this evening.'

'Right-ho. I'll be waiting on the mat,' said Grimsdyke submissively. 'About what time?'

'Not before one-thirty. Miss Fairchild is going to a supper party at *Les Ambassadeurs*.'

'And how's her second bottle of medicine going along?'

'It doesn't seem to taste at all like the first one, Dr Grimsdyke.'

'Oh, come come. The same prescription and all that. Perhaps Miss Fairchild's been eating something first—onions, or so on?'

'It is always *I* who tastes Miss Fairchild's medicines, Dr

Grimsdyke. Will you kindly send another prescription to her suite at once? And Miss Fairchild never eats onions.'

'You see the situation?' asked Grimsdyke as the girl left us. 'That's the secretary, of course. Absolutely under old Fairchild's thumb. And what's more, seems to revel in it. She's a psychologically negative personality, just the same as the husband. He's a rather nasty chap with Charing Cross Road hair, who spends his time trotting meekly after his illustrious missus helping her out of her minks and into her Rolls. What a life! But it brings me right to my point. Listen, old lad——'

He glanced round the bar again.

'You're sound on your professional secrecy, I suppose?'

'Of course I am!'

'Forgive my asking, but it's absolutely essential that not a word of this leaks out. Even to other members of the trade.' He dropped his voice further. 'I have reason to suspect that Miss Monica Fairchild is in the family way.'

I raised my eyebrows. 'Really? That'll be very interesting for everyone.'

'It certainly will be. If she *is*. After that bloomer on the high seas I'm not going to be caught a second time, believe me. Oh, no! That's why I wanted a consultation with you, with your up-to-the-minute experience of the condition.'

'What are her symptoms?' I asked.

After he had described them I agreed, 'It certainly sounds suspiciously like it.'

'Exactly, old lad. The question is, what's the next move?'

'Wouldn't it be simplest if you just sent her along to one of the high-powered gynae. boys in Harley Street?'

'That's the snag,' Grimsdyke explained, with a worried look. 'You can't imagine how tricky it is dealing with La

Fairchild. Why, I daren't even raise the subject. Oh, I know all about the doctor-patient relationship and so on. But none of the rules apply to this particular one. There'd be a tremendous fuss, to start with. And if I was wrong . . . Well, they wouldn't need a doctor, they'd need a lion-tamer.'

'Then if you want to make the diagnosis discreetly, why not fall back on our mutual friend the xenopus frog?' I suggested.

He looked puzzled. 'The what frog, old lad? I never was very hot on my midder and gynae.'

'It's the standard test,' I explained. 'All you do is acquire what is known generally to the public as "a speci-men." You send the bottle to the clever chaps in the path. lab., and by applying it to one of these unfortunate frogs they can tell in a few hours whether the patient is or isn't. It's all a matter of excreted hormones. Of course, it has to be a xenopus frog, which is also known as the *xenopus laevis*, or South African clawed toad——'

Grimsdyke jumped up.

'My dear chap, what a magnificent idea! I can easily get her to provide me with a specimen, without saying what it's for. Then I'll send it to the lab. and have the answer in my pocket with no one the wiser. That makes life ever so much simpler. I'll be eternally grateful to you.'

'Only too glad to help,' I said modestly.

'Look here, let me express my thanks in more useful form. Why don't you and Nikki come down to dinner one evening? Don't worry, it'll all come off the old expense sheet,' he added, as I hesitated. 'We can all three of us have an absolutely slap-up beano, completely buckshee. Yes, I'll get the chef to start laying it on straight away.' He rubbed his hands enthusiastically. 'Great chum of mine, the old chef, now I treat his chronic indigestion.'

'It's certainly very decent of you, Grim,' I told him appreciatively. 'I'm sure Nikki would like to come very much.'

'It's the least I can do, old lad. Though I'm afraid you'll have to dress up a bit,' he apologised. 'I have to change into a dinner jacket at nightfall, like a ruddy television announcer. Let's make it Wednesday fortnight.'

With strong feelings of mutual helpfulness, we parted.

'I'd simply love to go to the Arundel,' said Nikki, when I got home that night. 'It'll be quite a treat, particularly as we haven't been out for ages.'

'And particularly as it won't cost us a bean.'

'I shall need a new dress, of course, darling.'

'New dress? But what about that new black one you're so fond of?'

'Oh, but I couldn't possibly wear *that* at the Arundel.'

'Then I suppose I'd better get my dinner-jacket cleaned,' I grumbled. 'It's still wearing the battle scars of the last St Swithin's reunion.'

'Yes, it *will* be nice going out,' repeated Nikki. 'While I'm still fit to appear in public.'

6

About this time our unborn child introduced me to Dr Ann Pheasant, M.R.C.O.G.

Dr Pheasant was in practice on the other side of Hampden Cross, and being a member of the Royal College of Obstetricians and Gynaecologists—known in the trade as the royal college of organ-grinders—she attended most of the local confinements. I myself avoided maternity patients as shamelessly as smallpox cases, and now knew as little obstetrics as a retired surgeon-admiral. As Dr Farquarson really enjoyed delivering babies only by the light of guttering candles in a crofter's cottage during a Highland blizzard, Nikki herself performed most of the midwifery in our own practice, an arrangement which would have to be modified when she started to frighten all her new patients. But she had known the obstetrician since Dr Pheasant was a student senior to her in medical school, and she decided to place her own pregnancy in her hands.

'Of course, it's the best idea of the lot, pupping at home,' declared Dr Pheasant, sitting in our cottage on a social rather than professional visit. 'It pleases the pundits

in the Ministry of Health, who don't have to pay for
your board and lodging and clean sheets,' she went on.
'It's a jolly sight more convenient, and you can order
your own grub. For the mother's psychology you can't
beat it. You get an extra four quid out of the Government,
too.'

'I'd rather like to have it at home,' agreed Nikki.
'Hospitals these days seem to be getting as impersonal as
department stores.'

'And the father's always handy,' Ann continued warmly.
'Personally, I like to persuade him to watch the actual
delivery as well. Had to give the idea up, though. So many
of them were sick.'

'I'm quite certain I'd be,' I told her.

I never felt wholly at ease with Ann Pheasant. One
of the brightest splashes on the modern academic scene
is the discovery of professional women that asserting their
equality with men doesn't necessitate stripping themselves
of their sexual characteristics. Lady doctors, like lady
politicians and lady Wimbledon champions, now appear
in public looking pressingly feminine instead of going
about as if they had all been drawn by Mr James Thurber.
But some girls seem perpetually confused by the essentially
male world of medicine, and looking at Dr Ann Pheasant,
a cigarette dangling from her lips, clasping her knees
and showing her knickers, I felt that she was one of
them.

'Come along to the surgery and I'll do your haemo-
globin and blood pressure and albumin,' she went on,
slapping Nikki on the knee. 'And I must remember to give
you a certificate. In the eyes of the Welfare State you're
not officially pregnant without one. You can make up

your mind if you want to have it at home, or in the local Memorial Hospital or what have you, a bit later on.'

She got up.

'I must be nipping along to my other mothers. Give me a ring, old thing, and *relax*. Relaxation—that's the secret of modern childbirth. And do your exercises and watch your fat. Pregnant women put on an indecent amount of weight, quite apart from the little beast and its landing-tackle. Cheery-bye, and don't worry.'

'Dr Pheasant certainly brings a refreshingly basic approach to the miracle of childbirth,' I observed as she rattled away in her old car, which seemed to be held together largely with lengths of the surgical wire used to repair hernias.

'She's very sweet really, dear,' said Nikki.

I said nothing. A wife's friends are a mystery to any man.

'Particularly as I don't suppose there's much chance of her ever having a baby of her own,' Nikki added.

'But that ghastly idea of hers, having the husband in the room. I'm sure it's much better for everyone's psychology if he enjoys his traditional twilight sleep in the nearest pub. Anyway, where would you really like to have the baby? I suppose you're still not keen on St Swithin's?'

I had at first wanted the child to be born in the place which had provided me with my means of livelihood and most of my friends. There is a robust family spirit about all big British hospitals, where many of the staff take a wife from the nurses' home and a family from the obstetrical wards before ending up themselves on one of the porcelain tables in the post-mortem department.

The Maternity Department at St Swithin's seemed to be maintained exclusively for the convenience of its former pupils, and I knew that Sir Jeffrey Supe, the senior gynaecologist, would treat my application for a bed with the geniality shown by Harley-street consultants to all their old students, who might now be in a position to send them private patients.

But I knew that Turtle Supe, though a man who almost weekly presented Debrett with another entry, always seemed to be attending either a confinement in the country or Ascot races whenever he was wanted in a hurry. We decided that Nikki might end up anyway in the hands of Sister Studholm, the senior midwife, who was widely held to be a contemporary of Sarah Gamp and once reported me to the Dean for changing the 'e' on the Ante-Natal Clinic door to an 'i.'

'No, Simon,' Nikki now declared. 'Not St Swithin's. Apart from anything else—though as a primip. I suppose I can expect about twelve hours' warning—if anything went wrong it would be highly undignified for someone to be born along the North Circular Road. Let's have it at home. After all, a newborn baby hardly takes up more room than a puppy.'

'At this home?' I asked, looking round. I was fond of our cottage, but it was as draughty to live in as Stonehenge. 'Besides, we can't have the poor little thing sharing the camp-bed at week-ends with Grimsdyke.'

'Perhaps,' said Nikki doubtfully, 'the time has come for us to launch into something grander?'

'There goes the sports car,' I sighed. 'But I suppose a family man has to face a few necessary expenses.'

'By the way, talking of necessary expenses, dear,' Nikki

went on. 'That dress I bought for our party at the Arundel next week *was* rather more than we expected. And of course I had to get a new bag to go with the dress. And new shoes to go with the bag, and some more nylons to go with the shoes.'

I only hoped that Grimsdyke would put on a damn good menu.

I was looking forward to our outing not only for gustatory reasons but to discover the result of my friend's stealthy clinical investigations. But it was unnecessary to wait until then, for the next morning our paper exclaimed MONICA FAIRCHILD TO HAVE BABY. There was a long account on the front page, illustrated with a photograph of the actress gazing into the eyes of her husband, an under-nourished-looking young man with large eyes and a feathery moustache.

'Old Grim's got it right this time, anyway,' I announced to Nikki, tossing the paper across the kitchen table. 'I bet he's feeling pretty pleased with himself, even though they don't actually mention him by name.'

'But they mention the hotel, twice.'

'Perhaps they might let the poor chap keep a bit more of his own fees, now,' I suggested.

'Or give him a better job in the publicity department,' said Nikki.

Grimsdyke's increased importance in the Arundel as Monica Fairchild's prospective *accoucheur* was clear from the moment my car drew up at the front door the following Wednesday evening. The staff now bowed us in with the respectful curiosity shown these days only to royalty and television personalities.

'Nikki, my dear, you look absolutely charming,' said

Grimsdyke, greeting us exuberantly as we were shown up
to his suite by three pageboys. 'Hang up your hats and
we'll have a quick one first from my private cellar. I hope
you're both starving,' he went on. 'We're kicking off with
a mouthful of caviar, then a spot of soup and a chunk of
salmon just off the plane from Scotland, followed by a
duckling apiece done as the old chef used to produce it for
the aristocracy of Europe, when they could afford to eat
in places like this. And to save messing about with the
wine list, I've told them just to lay on bags of the bubbly
stuff.'

'Lovely!' said Nikki. She closed her eyes in contentment.
'I don't have to cook a bit of it myself.'

'Tell me, Grim,' I asked him, 'how in the end did you
manage your little deception with Miss Fairchild?'

'My dear chap, it was easier than testing her knee-jerks.
At our next consultation I simply put on a serious face and
told her what I wanted, and the next morning her secretary
brought it down in a Chanel perfume bottle. I sent it off
to the lab. in a taxi, and a couple of days later I got the
happy news.'

'Which you still had to break to the patient?'

'Exactly. That needed a bit of courage, I admit. But
there was nothing to be gained by beating about the
gooseberry bush. I kept quiet about my methods, naturally,
but I just drew a deep breath and told her. At first she
said, "Impossible! I'm on Broadway for the next six
months." But after that she saw things in the right per-
spective, and to my enormous relief threw herself head and
shoulders into the role of prospective mother. Jolly good at
it she is, too. And look how her audiences reacted! Why,
the day the newspapers gave it out they pretty well raised

the roof. She says her agent can get her another two and a half per cent on the strength of it.'

'I'm sure she looks just like anyone else when she's being sick in the mornings,' said Nikki, a little unkindly.

'And I hope she's now affording you the honour and gratitude you deserve?'

'My dear old lad, she's all over me. She calls me her "true apothecary"—*Romeo and Juliet*, you understand. More to the point, she's half-promised to take me to the States when she goes, presumably in the puerperium. That's the place to practice the healing art, and no mistake.'

He grinned enthusiastically, and emptied his glass.

'Great believers in science, the Yanks. They turn on medical advice like their bathwater. None of them would think of blowing their noses or changing the baby's nappies without first consulting the appropriate specialist —all American doctors of course being specialists. I tell them I'm a general specialist, and that seems to do the trick. If you'd like to go down and eat,' he added, glancing at his watch. 'With any luck we'll have a view of my distinguished patient as she sails out to perform.'

Grimsdyke seemed in great form. I couldn't remember seeing him so pleased with life since—to the equal surprise of the examiners and himself—he had passed his finals.

As it was early the dining-room was almost empty when we sat down at a special table heaped with flowers in the corner, heavily outnumbered by waiters. I was just eyeing the caviar glistening so expensively before me, when Grimsdyke gave a nudge and whispered, 'Here she comes now.'

I had seen Monica Fairchild before only on the stage,

where her personality filled the theatre like some powerful gas bursting into a vacuum. I could now tell instantly from the set of her blonde head and blue eyes that it was not simply a stage presence, which seemed confirmed by the look of the husband plodding dejectedly behind her.

'She's coming across for a word,' continued Grimsdyke excitedly. 'Would you like to be introduced?'

'We certainly wouldn't want to complicate——' began Nikki.

'Dear Dr Grimsdyke,' declared the actress, advancing on our table. 'I just wanted to tell you that I am *quite all right*. I thought you might be worrying.'

'I'm delighted to hear it, Miss Fairchild,' exclaimed Grimsdyke, jumping up. 'And now may I have the pleasure of introducing two of my professional colleagues and personal friends—Dr and Mrs Sparrow.'

'How do you do?' said Miss Fairchild, as though we were in the back of the gallery.

'As a matter of fact,' went on Grimsdyke, rather carried away by the occasion, 'I might as well confess now, Miss Fairchild, that I called Dr Sparrow here into consultation to discuss how we could diagnose your present happy condition.'

'I've often wondered, Doctor,' her husband interjected to prevent himself being totally ignored, 'how your profession *does* manage to diagnose these things?'

'Oh, it was quite simple from the contents of that perfume bottle,' I replied without thinking.

The actress frowned slightly.

'What is this, Dr Grimsdyke?'

Grimsdyke shot me a glance.

'Well, you see Miss Fairchild,' he said quickly. 'That—

er, what you kindly let me have, was taken to the laboratory, and they sent me back the result. Didn't I tell you?'

'Do you imagine, young man,' she declared in the voice of Cleopatra, 'that for one moment I would allow you to submit me to such an indignity? Of course not!'

Grimsdyke suddenly looked worried.

'You mean that—that offering wasn't exactly—er, yours?'

'I shouldn't think of it! No more than I'd give away locks of my own hair for the hundreds of demands that come every post.'

'Good God!' said Grimsdyke, grasping the table. 'Then you're not——'

'*What* are you trying to say, you fool?' thundered Miss Fairchild.

'Perhaps my diagnosis was a little exaggerated,' muttered Grimsdyke, staring at me hopelessly.

'If you are trying to infer,' Miss Fairchild flashed at him, 'that I am *not* going to have a baby, that is completely out of the question. It's already been announced in the newspapers.'

'But Miss Fairchild,' I interrupted bravely, to save my friend, 'How on earth could you have obtained such an appropriate specimen otherwise?'

'As it all seemed of no importance,' she snapped at me, 'I got my secretary to supply it.'

There was a loud cry behind her and a crash.

'My God!' screamed the actress. 'Fetch a doctor! Rollo's dead!'

But her husband had only fainted.

'I've never been treated like this in my life,' declared

Grimsdyke indignantly, as the three of us stood outside on the pavement. 'I didn't even have the chance to swallow a single ruddy sturgeon's egg. And telling the valet to pack my things, too! I'm damn well going to sue that manager. You wait and see. I'll go to my solicitors first thing in the morning.'

'I'd hold your horses a bit, if I were you,' I told him sympathetically. 'He might be able to sue you.'

Grimsdyke stood glaring for some moments at the site of his former employment.

'Oh, well,' he grunted. 'I've been thrown out of better places than this. Anyway, there's plenty of spots we can go and dine—the Ritz, Mirabelle, Mayfair——'

His voice trailed off as he remembered that he didn't have an expense account at any of them.

'I don't suppose you could lend me a few quid, old lad?' he asked. 'I'm a bit short.'

'I'm awfully sorry, Grim. But in the circumstances I didn't bother to bring my wallet.'

'I've got a little loose change if it's any help,' said Nikki, opening her bag.

We managed to raise eight and tenpence between us.

'We can run to half a pint in the nearest pub, I suppose,' said Grimsdyke, pocketing it. 'Then there's a fish and chip parlour I know off the Edgware Road. I never did care for rich food much, anyway.'

7

AFTER the unfortunate evening at the Arundel Grimsdyke seemed to disappear. In the expectation of living in rent-free luxury he had sublet his Chelsea flat to a visiting Australian neurologist, and at St Swithin's —which he regarded primarily as his London club, dropping in to read the common-room papers and chat to his old friends—no one heard of him for several weeks. Meanwhile, the press announced that Miss Monica Fairchild was 'taking a prolonged rest from the stage on the advice of her doctors.'

'I don't know who her doctors are,' I remarked to Nikki over breakfast. 'But I know one doctor who certainly isn't.'

'Poor Grimsdyke! Do you suppose he's really gone on that Antarctic whaling expedition?'

'I must say the other night he seemed pretty serious about not looking at a woman for the next six months. Though I can hardly imagine him as a sort of Moby Doc.'

'I do wish he'd take up something completely unromantic, like public health,' sighed Nikki. 'Even he couldn't get into much trouble with dustbins and drains.'

'I wouldn't be too sure about that.'

As the weeks went by I began to feel genuinely anxious about him. Grimsdyke was such a social being that he would have found himself unable to keep away from his old friends and old haunts even if he had just committed a murder. I wondered seriously if he had emigrated to start practice in New Zealand, or was perhaps officiating somewhere more inaccessible as an original type of medical missionary.

It was then the middle of July, and when I took a day off to watch the Gentlemen *versus* Players match at Lord's I looked for him in the Tavern, which is one of those places like the Royal Academy and Piccadilly Circus Tube Station where you often run into people you want to see— as well as many that you don't.

I didn't find Grimsdyke but I found news of him, from another former classmate at St Swithin's, Tony Benskin.

'Grimsdyke?' he said. 'Yes, I came across him a week or so back, when I was in Simpson's buying some socks.'

We were standing on the Tavern steps with pints of beer in the mild afternoon sunshine, watching the English captain score an elegant century.

'He was fitting himself out with tropical kit,' Tony went on. 'You know, Boy Scout shorts and mosquito nets and so forth. I asked where he was off to, but he seemed pretty cagey about it all. Only said something about having to be out of the country for a bit. A woman as usual, I suppose?'

'Well, it's a woman. But not as usual.'

'I envy the chap, in a way. With his ideas of practice he may not see much medicine, but he certainly sees plenty of life. Oh, good shot, sir!' he said, as the ball rattled against the boundary boards. 'Anything exciting happening to you?'

'Yes, we're having a baby,' I said proudly.

'Oh, really? We're having our fourth.'

'Your *fourth*! Good God, man, have you found out what's causing it?'

'You must come back and meet the family at the close of play,' he invited. 'I might be able to give you a few tips on practical fatherhood.'

The Benskins lived in Hampstead, and were one of those disorganised households who always seem to have twice as many children as they really possess. When I arrived it was bedtime, and they appeared to have a small school on their hands.

'I suppose you've read von Schaeffer's book on *The Importance of Antenatal Influences on the Developing Subconscious*?' Tony Benskin asked, pouring me a drink over the heads of his two oldest, who were sitting on their pots in front of the fireplace while the third screamed off-stage being put to bed.

'I don't think I've even heard of it, I'm afraid.'

'My dear chap,' he insisted. 'Every father in the country should be made to read it from cover to cover. To my mind, bringing up children is a highly scientific process, right from the moment of conception. Molly disagreed with me at first, but I've talked her round to my way of thinking. Our children have everything from a meta-bolically-adjusted diet to psychologically-adjusted colours in their bedroom. Absolutely essential to remember details like that. Otherwise they might easily get stuck in the stage of oral eroticism for ever.'

'Perhaps for the first one we'll keep to the old blue-for-a-boy and pink-for-a-girl stuff,' I told him doubtfully.

'Do you realise every male child wants to emasculate its father for being in love with its mother?' Tony demanded.

I looked alarmed. 'But they don't, very often, surely?'

'A subconscious thought, of course,' he explained. 'Then there's the interesting condition of the couvade——'

Unable to help laughing any longer, I exclaimed, 'Surely, Tony! Even you must admit that the husband sharing the wife's symptoms is all a bit of an old wives' tale?'

'There are more things in heaven and earth, Horatio, than are dreamt of in Eden and Holland's *Manual of Obstetrics*,' he told me darkly. 'Whenever Molly goes into labour I get the most shocking bellyache.'

'As a matter of fact, I did feel a bit sick in the mornings myself earlier on,' I admitted. 'But I put that down to Grimsdyke's bottle of duty-free rum.'

'It's all very well for him to talk,' said Molly Benskin, when a few minutes later I congratulated her on such enlightened parenthood, while Tony took his turn putting the other two psychological problems to bed.

'He hasn't got to wash the nappies,' she went on, pouting. 'Or do the ironing and mop up the puddles and wipe their beastly little faces every couple of minutes from morning to night. The amount of money Tony wastes on books about child psychology would buy me a washing machine, which would be a hundred times as useful. There's only one thing I know for certain about child psychology,' she ended despondently, 'that whatever you do, it's bound to be wrong.'

'If I can speak from purely theoretical experience, I'm inclined to agree with you.'

'There's only one way to prepare a child for life,' Molly Benskin said firmly. 'Stand him on a high shelf, open your arms, and say "Jump." Then walk away. I wish to heaven

Tony would mess about with the car instead, like any normal man.'

But my visit to the Benskins was useful, because it left me with feelings that I was perhaps not taking my coming responsibilities seriously enough. And my concern was less with the psychological sufferings of our unborn infant than finding somewhere for the poor thing eventually to live.

'Either everyone's become so attached to Hampden Cross they don't want to leave the damn place,' I told Nikki, 'or someone's discovered uranium in the garden and is secretly buying up the whole district.'

I had been window-shopping in estate agents', as I had done before we were married, though aware that I was now tied to an even less flexible time-table.

'There just doesn't seem to be anything suitable at all,' I complained. 'Can't you go into a few agents' offices yourself, now you're looking so earnestly pregnant?'

My wife had passed the depressing point when further struggle with ordinary clothes becomes hopeless, and had assumed the expectant mother's robes of office.

'I did, dear, this afternoon. But there were two others there already, both much further gone than me.'

'Then there'll be furniture, too,' I said sombrely. Although bank managers, building societies, and even bookies have a touching faith in the solvency of junior members of the medical profession, this was an item to be faced with respect. 'We've got the essentials, I suppose, what with wedding presents and so on, and we can always scrounge from our families. But we'll soon have to choose between next year's holiday and a contemporary sofa, even if we do find somewhere to put it.'

'Do you suppose one of the patients might be of help?'

'Old Mrs Mackinnon is looking a bit dickey. With a change in the weather there might be a vacancy there.'

'No,' said Nikki, with a shudder.

Shortly afterwards our problem was in fact solved by the misfortune of one of my patients, though luckily a less drastic one than Mrs Mackinnon's. I was still wondering if we might find a place going cheap with some fairly tolerable inconvenience like bad drains or poltergeists, when Major Marston appeared in the surgery complaining of giddy turns and hot feelings in the back of his head.

Major Marston was a man with pale blue eyes, a crumb-brush moustache, and a fondness for club cuff-links and suede boots, whom Nikki and I knew socially as well as professionally. He had a seat on the Town Council and was a prosperous Hampden Cross builder, which was widely held to be a matter of cause and effect. He lived with his pretty red-headed wife in a modern house on the far edge of the town, with two poodles and two television sets, all four of which they seemed extremely fond of. We had been to several of their cocktail parties—they were the leaders of the Hampden Cross set of bright middle-aged things—and I was now surprised when he confessed in response to a little elementary psychoanalysis that his wife had packed up and left him.

'One's simply got to face it, Doc,' he said. He squared the shoulders of his blazer. 'Diane prefers the other chap—no names, if you'll excuse me—and there it is. It's only life. We're being utterly sensible about the whole thing, of course. What else can one do? I'm going away for a bit of a holiday. To forget, if I can.'

'It'll certainly do the headaches good, at any rate.'

'Afterwards I'll move into one of the new flats we're

c

putting up, I suppose. I can't go on living where I am. Not among all the things I've provided her with, all reminding me so much——'

He expressed emotion by briskly wiping invisible froth from his moustache.

'Look here,' I said quickly, 'I don't want to interfere in your affairs, and certainly I don't want to cash in on your unhappiness, and this is probably highly unprofessional anyway, but . . . well, if you'd like to let the house furnished for a bit, we'd be very glad to take it.'

'That's very decent of you,' he said, after the natural hesitation of a man passing objects of sentimental value into the hands of comparative strangers. 'As a matter of fact, I did hear a rumour you were looking for a place.'

To my delight he quickly agreed.

'You'll be quite discreet about it, Doc?' he asked, as we settled terms. 'I don't want anything like this buzzed about too much. Bad for business.'

'I won't say a word more than necessary, I assure you. And here's a prescription for some phenobarbitone—it might ease the strain a bit.'

'But it's absolutely marvellous!' said Nikki, when I told her. 'At least it'll give us a comfortable breathing space.'

'And now we can perfectly well have the baby at home. Even if the home isn't our own.'

Nikki hesitated. 'I suppose it's all—well, all right?'

'All right? But why on earth shouldn't it be all right?'

'I mean, it all seemed to be done so casually. Didn't he want an inventory or anything?'

'Oh, the poor chap was far too upset to go through all their belongings. And he said agreements and so on only made money for the lawyers—after all, he's a builder, and he ought to know. We just shook hands like gentlemen, and I gave him a cheque for the first quarter's rent.'

'It's all just a little odd to my female intuition,' said Nikki, frowning slightly.

'It isn't to mine. Not after the way we've seen that woman carry on at their parties. She really was a terrible flirt, you know. Remember that embarrassing business with the hardware dealer chap? And she *is* very attractive.'

'She's certainly very *slim*,' said Nikki, looking longingly in the direction of her own waist.

'Anyway,' I concluded. 'Let's be selfish and hope they don't have a reconciliation.'

I didn't see Major Marston again. He sent the keys to me that evening by post. A few days later we moved in, losing our own few pieces of furniture among our landlord's.

'I'm afraid I can't manage to carry you over the threshold,' I apologised to Nikki. 'But at least you've got nothing more to worry about except sitting patiently and knitting little things.'

But we had hardly arrived in our new home when our coming baby attracted attention from a wholly unexpected direction.

8

I RECOGNISED at once the bold sweep of the black ink on the envelope automatically redirected by the Post Office.

'It's from my godfather,' I exclaimed over the breakfast table. 'And the old boy hasn't so much as sent us a Christmas card since we were married.'

With interest sufficiently strong to be confessed as excitement, I opened the letter from Sir Lancelot Spratt, K.B.E., M.C., D.Sc., M.S., F.R.C.S.

> *Evan's Farm,*
> *Much Chilvers,*
> *Herefordshire.*

Dear Sparrow, (Sir Lancelot regarded Christian names as suitable only for addressing children and dogs.)

Your father spent a few days with me recently. I learn that your wife is shortly expecting a child. I am disappointed that you did not inform me of this, though not pained— after all, I am now an old man of little use to the world, finishing my days as untroublesomely as possible in the country. But I have something of importance in mind concerning your future infant, or infants. You will kindly meet me at the Parthenon at four o'clock next Monday afternoon. My regards.

L. S.

'He's actually coming to London,' I announced in surprise. 'After he swore he'd never set foot in the place again as long as he lived.'

Nikki looked alarmed. 'Oh, dear! I'll have to meet him.'

'He's not really so bad as everyone makes out,' I reassured her. 'All these old hospital figures are half-myth and half-monster.'

'So's the Abominable Snowman, but I wouldn't like to meet him either.'

'It's a pity you got him in your surgery finals, dear. Though he was probably only putting on a fierce face to convince himself that he wouldn't be influenced by a pretty one. He's really only a paper dragon.'

'Perhaps so, Simon. But at the time the smoke and flames seemed realistic enough. And it's going to be very awkward for you to go to London on Monday.'

'It would be very much more awkward for me if I didn't,' I told her.

I had not seen my godfather since he retired from the surgical staff of St Swithin's two years before, an event which had the same impact on the hospital as the Duke of Wellington's funeral on Victorian London. On his last operating afternoon I had joined his fellow surgeons and physicians gathered in the draughty Founders' Hall to present him with his portrait—a representation in scarlet robes, holding a skull, and wearing an expression of serenity observable in life only while sleeping through his colleagues' ceremonial lectures.

It was an occasion of genuine sadness both for his friends who referred to him as 'A Rembrandt of the Scalpel' and for his enemies, who referred to him as 'Old Blood and Thunder.' For thirty years Sir Lancelot had a say in

everything at St Swithin's from the choice of a new consultant to the choice of a new floor polish, until he thought
getting his own way there as natural as the law of gravity
and just as convenient for the orderly planning of human
affairs; but he was the last of the surgical generation
which once strode so largely down the stony Edwardian
corridors, whose love of his hospital was less only than his
love of his country and his family (indeed it often exceeded
the last when Lady Spratt was having one of her difficult
turns). He was a man too big for the age when British
consultants resemble the Civil Servants they so often fear
they are becoming.

'It is almost fifty years since I first came here,' Sir
Lancelot ended a dignified speech that afternoon describing the changes he had seen in St Swithin's, in tones
only faintly suggesting that most of them were for the
worse.

'I was a frightened student with a second-hand anatomy
book under my arm, and my only luggage was a dissecting
set and a blue serge suit—both, I confess, the property of
my father. After so long it is hard to believe that the time
has really come for us to part. But it has, and let us have
no sentimentality about it.

'I have now only one wish—to be remembered among
you in the words of the immortal Horace, *Integer vitae
scelerisque purus*—"He that is unstained in life and pure from
guilt." '

He dropped his voice. For once he made the translation
sound an afterthought instead of a condemnation of the
appalling lack of classical knowledge among modern
doctors.

'As for my own plans,' he concluded, 'I intend to pass

such days as the Lord may be pleased to spare me living
quietly on my estate in Herefordshire. In the country, with
my library, my casebooks, and above all my memories, I
shall at last have an opportunity to *contemplate*—an exercise
impossible, ladies and gentlemen, when you exhaust the
days and energies of a lifetime chasing pathology all round
the abdomen.'

'And guineas all over London,' muttered someone at
the back.

So Sir Lancelot disappeared from St Swithin's, to
expend his undiminished vigour on growing fruit and
treating Lady Spratt's lumbago. As his Rolls drove for the
last time from the hospital courtyard, with its few plane
trees blackened by the London fogs and its pair of statues
whitened by the London pigeons, and carried him through
gates where he could remember patients being borne on
window-shutters and consultants clattering up in a coach-
and-pair, everyone felt that he was vanishing into the
mists of medical mythology.

And with any luck they wouldn't hear of him again till
his memorial service.

Sir Lancelot's evacuation of the surgical battlefields on
which he had won and lost so many spectacular actions
still caused arguments at St Swithin's, being variously put
down to the threat of bronchitis or the threat of blackmail.
As an emeritus surgeon he could have commanded many
privileges, from offering his opinions on baffling cases to
enjoying his lunch in the hospital refectory, and several
old consultants continued to haunt the wards until they
slipped almost unnoticeably under one of the bed-covers
themselves.

'I refuse to play Ancient Mariner of the surgical seas,'

was all he replied when questioned. 'Besides, it's tediously simple being an emeritus consultant—there are sufficient people underneath to make all the mistakes first.'

It was therefore with much curiosity the following Monday that I put on my best suit and a stiff white collar and drove down to London to meet him, with feelings in my stomach that I remembered from the mornings before my *viva voce* examinations as a student.

The Parthenon was Sir Lancelot's club in St James's, and like everything else about him the grandest and most distinguished available. I knew nothing about London clubs, except the ones Grimsdyke took me to where blondes played pianos in the basement, but the Parthenon struck me as a series of long gloomy rooms filled with long gloomy armchairs in which long gloomy gentlemen sat asleep.

'Sir?' asked the porter.

I gave Sir Lancelot's name, feeling like Hamlet asking if his father's ghost were in.

'Sir Lancelot is expecting you in the morning room, sir.'

I had a moment of panic wondering how warmly I should greet my godfather. He was a man who became as uncomfortable in the presence of emotions as Napoleon was said to be in the presence of cats. But Sir Lancelot solved the problem by merely glancing up and saying, 'Have some tea, Sparrow,' as though I had slipped outside for a few minutes.

I had found him in morning clothes and cravat, eating hot buttered crumpets from a dish warmed with a small tank of hot water, spreading them alternately with straw-berry jam and Gentleman's Relish. I obediently took a large black leather armchair opposite.

'You're looking very well, sir,' I began politely.

'I *am* very well. I can walk three miles before breakfast and finish *The Times* crossword while I'm eating it. Can you? William, another tea, if you please.'

There was a short silence.

'Don't sit on the edge of your chair, boy. You're not a schoolgirl with an adolescent lordosis.'

'It's a pity you had to retire, sir,' I said, rearranging myself.

'It's a pity any of us have to retire. Why a man should be considered capable of performing major abdominal surgery the day before his sixty-fifth birthday, and incapable of anything except a little gentle gardening the day after, is totally beyond my comprehension.'

I agreed with him.

'And as usual, Sparrow, the medical profession's handed the dirty end of the stick. Look at the judges, sitting up there mumbling into their wigs till they're ninety. I'll wager half the bishops in the Establishment are too arthritic to get up the pulpit steps. And if you want a perfect study in senility take the House of Lords—which I ought to know, I've seen inside a good many of 'em. But with us it's all out at sixty-five, whatever the state of your brains or your blood pressure. That's the trouble with the modern world, there's no scope for individuality. God knows what would have happened to Leonardo da Vinci today. Got run in for breaking the Anatomy Acts for a start, I suppose.'

I could see that my godfather hadn't changed.

'Are you enjoying life in the country, sir?' I asked timidly, as the club butler shuffled up with my tea.

'I don't believe you can enjoy life anywhere these days, when it's easier to live like a saint than live like a gentleman. You mustn't smoke because it gives you cancer of the lungs, you mustn't eat because it gives you obesity and heart-attacks, and you mustn't drink because it's too damn expensive. And the only time I hear of my friends is when I read their obituaries in the *B.M.J.*'

He wiped his fingers on a yellow silk handkerchief.

'What's going on in Town?' he asked abruptly.

After chatting for a while about such things as the promenade concerts and test-matches, I asked guardedly how long he intended to stay. I felt it would be a matter of interest to anyone I met in St Swithin's.

'I've a few errands to do,' he said, seeming disinclined to answer. 'The missus wants some more dried ginger and belladonna plasters and so on. But I didn't ask you here for social gossip. I wish to have a serious and confidential talk with you, Sparrow. Don't worry about the feller in gaiters,' he added, noticing my glance towards a nearby chair. 'Deaf as a post for years.'

Sir Lancelot sat for some moments stroking his beard.

'I have never been a particularly conscientious godfather to you,' he declared to my surprise. 'I don't mind telling you I only took on the job because your father was my house-surgeon. I didn't have time to do much about it. I didn't have time to do much about anything, it's beginning to strike me,' he went on reflectively. 'As a busy surgeon you have to hurry through life with one eye on your watch, like the White Rabbit. Also, I thought you were a bit of a fool,' he added amiably. 'But I suppose you got in with the wrong set—that Grimsdyke, and suchlike. Which is why I'm particularly gratified that at last you've settled down like a responsible member of society and started a family.'

'Very kind of you to say so, sir,' I murmured.

'As you know,' he continued, taking no notice of my remark. 'I have neither children, nephews, nieces, cousins, pet dogs, parrots, nor leanings towards the Medical Benevolent Fund. Whatever you hear at the hospital, I've never been a particularly rich man. But I was brought up in the house of a mine-workers' G.P. on Tyneside, where to avoid suffering from mass nutritional deficiency we had to keep a watch on every ha'penny, and the habit stuck. So a few years ago I found that I could endow a few scholarships at St Swithin's.'

We were interrupted by an elderly member who murmured as he passed, 'Afternoon, Spratt. Been away?'

'Did his right inguinal hernia five years ago,' explained Sir Lancelot, glancing after him keenly. 'Now it looks as if the other side's coming down. Do you know, I've spotted two emphysemas and a spondylitis since lunch? Veritable mines of pathology, these old London clubs. But I digress.'

He lay back and placed together the thin finger-tips that had explored ten thousand abdomens.

'Do you know why I left London?' he demanded.

'To follow the example of Candide, sir?' I suggested.

'I assure you I should much rather have followed the example of a brewer's drayhorse and died in harness. In short, I was disgusted at the way St Swithin's treated me.'

As I looked surprised, he explained, 'I had been promised—or almost promised—an official letter inviting me to stay on the staff till the hospital bicentenary next year. All I got was a chit from the administrative officer—that beastly little man I hadn't spoken to for years—reminding me to leave the keys of my locker before departing. After half a century I was kicked out like one of the surgery porters. There's socialised medicine for you.'

He paused to blow his nose wrathfully.

'You'll keep quiet about all this?' he asked with a sharp glance.

'I should certainly be most discreet about your affairs, sir.'

'I'm glad to hear it, because otherwise I'd break your neck. You know me, Sparrow. I never do things by halves. I'm either in or out. And I was out. So I wrote to my patients to close down my practice in London, and to my agent to open up my place in Hereford. And here we are.'

I said nothing, knowing what a painful self-amputation it must have been. But like all good surgeons, Sir Lancelot was an incorrigible exhibitionist.

After searching for some consoling remark I told him, 'Everyone at St Swithin's has missed you very much.'

Sir Lancelot seemed amused. 'My dear feller, one half of the staff could hardly wait to get rid of me, and the other half has been expecting me to drop dead for years. You can't imagine how demoralising it is to find your junior colleagues inspecting you over lunch for the first signs of arteriosclerosis, cerebral softening, and general decay and ruin. But the net result is no scholarships for St Swithin's.'

He paused as the arthritic butler appeared to gather our tea things.

'Instead,' Sir Lancelot went on, 'I intend to educate the brood of the devil I know. I'm not aware how many children you intend to have, Sparrow, but I'm going to settle some cash on 'em. Don't thank me,' he said quickly, seeming alarmed at the possibility. 'I distrust gratitude

almost as much as I distrust flattery. Save a man's life and
he complains the stitches tickle and your bill's too high.
Do something in five minutes for his piles or his flat feet
and you've got a devoted friend for life. Besides,' he added
after a moment, 'if you don't get it, the tax merchants will.'

He gave a short laugh.

'I remember when the old Duke of Helford fell off his
horse, they sent for his accountants before they sent for his
doctors. It was myself who pulled him through in the end.
Then he went and got married again to some young chit
and blewed the lot. Family hasn't spoken to me since. I'm
coming to see what sort of a home you run, Sparrow.
What's the address again? I shall arrive next Tuesday
week after luncheon, and I shall be staying the night.'

9

I DROVE home in some confusion. I had no head for finance and figures, unlike Grimsdyke, who could work out such things as daily doubles and tote accumulators without bothering to use a pencil. I realised that my godfather's gift would have to be put to the most solemn use, but I couldn't help myself feeling that somewhere might be the chance to order a new sports car. On the whole, I felt like Pip in *Great Expectations*.

I was just preparing to startle Nikki with the news, when I turned into our road and noticed Grimsdyke's Bentley drawn up at the front gate. A few minutes later I found him sunburnt and cheerful in the sitting-room, sitting in my chair with his feet on the fireplace drinking my beer.

'Why on earth didn't you tell me you'd moved?' he demanded almost at once. 'Gave me quite a nasty turn seeing the "SOLD" sign on your old habitat. I went mooching round the district for hours, until I had enough sense to ring up the local Executive Council and get your phone number.'

'How could we tell you, when we didn't know where you were yourself?' protested Nikki, appearing with another couple of bottles of beer.

'What, didn't I let you know I'd cleared off to the West Indies?'

'Not on another cruise?' I exclaimed.

'Good God, no! Things were pretty bad after the Fairchild episode, but they weren't as bad as that. As a matter of fact, I've been in the oil business. But I hear you've been bearding Sir Lancelot, you brave chap. And how is the old blunderbuss?'

'In very good form. By the way, he seemed to remember you.'

'I should think he does. In my time as a student he threw pretty well everything movable in the theatre at me, except the patient. But what on earth brings him back to London?'

'Oh, nothing in particular,' I said. I felt it unwise even to hint at our conversation before such an enthusiastic gossip as Grimsdyke. 'But tell us what you've been up to yourself. The way you go shooting off to the ends of the earth makes you look like Edmund Hillary to stay-at-homes like us.'

'It's very simple, actually.' Grimsdyke opened another bottle of beer. 'After that ghastly evening in the Arundel —I'll stand you the dinner I owe you, by the by, I'm in the chips again—I felt the time had come for me to be out of the country for a bit. Awkward questions might be asked in theatrical circles. As a matter of fact my exit went smoothly. Although my own professional qualifications may not, I fear, be of the best, I have one great advantage in the medical labour market—will go anywhere and do anything. When you come to think of it, there aren't many doctors without a regular job and a regular wife, however fed up they may get from time to time with either.'

I agreed with him.

'After we left that fish-shop I spent the night in the Turkish bath, and the next morning went back to the Arundel to collect my belongings. There I ran into that American you met—Mr McGlew.'

'You mean the pork chap?'

Grimsdyke nodded.

'He immediately sensed something was up, doubtless because I was wandering about in full evening dress while everyone else was eating bacon and eggs. So I told him pretty tersely how I'd been chucked out. He became very sympathetic, because I think he'd rather taken to me— which proves what a good thing it is to cast your bread upon the waters, even when you think the tide's never going out.

'As I believe I told you, like most Yanks chum McGlew imagined that once he'd left behind his air-conditioning and automatic Martini mixer he'd said good-bye to civilisation. When he sent for a doctor in London I really believe he half-expected someone to show up with monkey skulls round his waist and a horn of powdered snake-tooth. But knowing a thing or two, I borrowed the barman's jacket and looked at his tongue with a head mirror, just like the doctors in advertisements advising people to choke themselves to death with cigarettes.

'That did the trick, all right,' Grimsdyke told us with satisfaction. 'McGlew just sat back and let me take charge of his complaints. And he'd got hundreds of them, probably all caught from the *Reader's Digest*. He also insisted on paying enough per visit to keep a British family ill in comfort for a couple of years.

'Like most Americans, old McGlew was a generous soul,

and he was also very keen on democratic justice. So on hearing the story of my high-handed dismissal he insisted on finding me another job at once—he's not only in pigs, you know, he's in oil, and it must be awfully monotonous for him turning up year after year in the list of the world's ten richest chaps. Anyway, he's got a tame oil company in London, and there and then he rang up the managing director and told him he was sending me along.

'This oil company had an office near the Guildhall, and about the same size. The managing director turned out to be a genial cove, who gave me a cigar and summoned the company secretary, who summoned the chief medical officer. Cash means nothing to these petrol boys, of course,' Grimsdyke explained authoritatively. 'They could employ pretty well the whole B.M.A. on what the public puts in its lighters.

'The chief M.O. said as a matter of fact they did want someone, to go at once to Poparapetyl. The company's regular doctor there was on a month's leave, which apparently didn't usually matter but some big bug with one of the most expensive blood pressures in the New York office had just gone snooping round the place. I accepted the locum on the spot, and they all looked delighted. Though whether through concern over this chap's blood pressure or doing the bidding of old McGlew without busting themselves, I wouldn't like to say.

'The managing director then gave me another cigar and added that if I liked the job they'd be happy to keep me on the regular pay-roll. So when the next morning I found myself at London Airport with a bag of brand-new tropical kit and a whacking great cheque in my pocket, it put my morale up no end.'

'Where on earth's Poparapetyl?' asked Nikki. 'It sounds like some sort of bacterium.'

'I hardly knew myself till I got there. It's an island about the size of Anglesey off the coast of Venezuela, and it consists largely of oil derricks, Coca-Cola signs, and chaps in coloured shirts asleep under carts. Also, it is damned hot.

'I arrived from Caracas in a small plane, and took an old taxi from the airstrip to the oil company's bungalows —all very white and neat, and looking the cross between a holiday camp and a municipal sanatorium.

'There didn't seem to be anyone about, and I didn't blame them in that heat, which was enough to raise blisters on a set of snooker balls. So I woke up the amiable Poparapetylian who seemed to be the chief turnkey, and explained that I was the new doctor. He seemed rather surprised, but he showed me to the bungalow with "DOCTOR" on the door and went back to sleep again. And thus I took up the White Man's Burden. Have you got any more beer? The very thought of the place makes me thirsty.'

'I believe there's some in the new fridge,' said Nikki. 'Though as I haven't got the hang of the switches yet you may have to eat it with a hammer and chisel.'

'However hot the climate, it doesn't sound a bad job at all,' I told him as I refilled his tankard. 'If the pay was good you might have done worse than sticking it out for a year or so.'

'The very same thoughts passed through my mind, old lad, as I dumped my duffle-bag on the bunk and switched on the radio, water-cooler, and air-conditioning. Oil's all very well, but you have to go to such beastly places to get it that the companies pamper their servants a bit. I could have lived in modest comfort until everyone had forgotten about the Fairchild, even if she certainly hadn't forgotten about me. But,' Grimsdyke continued solemnly, 'within a short hour or so such ideas were squashed for good and all.'

'That sounds very alarming,' said Nikki.

'It was alarming. Though it was perhaps for the best. If the horrible dangers of the place had been brought home to me years later it might have been a shattered Grimsdyke that walked through your door, with his liver jostling with his appendix for room in his pelvis.'

'You mean drink?' I asked simply.

He nodded.

'We all like a glass or two and no harm done. Particularly in this part of the world where you know what you're getting, even if it is labelled something like MacEuston Scotch. Not so at Poparapetyl.'

My friend paused to reflect.

'The first thing I wanted when I arrived, naturally, was a noggin. So I wandered into the sunshine, and noticing a signpost labelled "To the Capital" I followed it.

'After a short but highly thirst-making walk I reached the place, which consisted of a mixture of huts and telegraph poles and was made largely out of old oil drums. But in the middle stood a more solid-looking structure labelled "Savoy Hotel," and I felt that even out of homesickness I had to go in.

'The Savoy wasn't much like the original, of course. But I went through a door like the ones you see chaps getting chucked out of in Wild West films, and found myself in a dim little bar which was at least a bit cooler than outside. Behind the bar was another Poparapetylian with his head in his hands asleep—which seems to be the great national enthusiasm—and in front of it was a soldierly-looking old boy with a spiky moustache and a dirty white suit.

' "Why, if it isn't old Bill Mackenzie!" he said as soon as I came in. "After all these years! I suppose you've just arrived in this incestuous hell-hole from London?"

' "I've certainly just come from London, my dear sir," I told him. "But I'm equally certain I'm not anyone called——"

' "Dear old Bill!" the chap insisted. "We've certainly got to have a drink on it. George! Double rum swizzle for my old friend Bill Mackenzie, pronto."

'I thought he might be a bit myopic or something, but further explanations were prevented by my sipping the rum swizzle. You know I've always been rather partial to a drop of rum? I regarded it as nice bland stuff you pour over Christmas puddings. I took a large gulp, and made a noise like a chap on the wrong end of Sir Lancelot's gastroscope. Phew! It pretty well ripped the epithelium off my oesophagus.

' "The drinks out here take a little getting used to," said the soldierly chap, patting me hard on the back. "But even in the old days, Bill, you had a weak head for the drink, eh? And for the women, too, ha ha! Why, it must be years since we strolled together on a Saturday night to Frascati's. How's the dear Alhambra going along?"

'I was just going to tell him that I knew about as much of the dear Alhambra as of the Great Exhibition of 1851, when he started picking threads from the sleeve of his jacket. At least, I thought he was, until he began chucking them on to the floor and grinding them under his foot.

' "Do these little green lizards we have out here worry you much?" he asked in a friendly sort of way.

'Then, of course, I made the diagnosis. Mental confusion, loss of memory for recent events, hallucinations—the chap was a roaring alcoholic. You never see a case like it in England. It's much too expensive a disease for the inhabitants.

' "Do you—er, drink very much?" I enquired, as casually as possible.

' "Alas!" replied the old boy. "I am a martyr to it. Have another." '

10

'THINGS then started to get rather difficult,' Grimsdyke
went on.

I was wondering how our education at St Swithin's
had equipped him to manage this problem of practical
medicine.

'You know what it's like dealing with one of these cases,
Simon? Just the same as playing with a pet tiger. They're
all very nice and friendly, but you can't be too certain
when they're going to bite your head off.

'A chronic alcoholic not being the most suitable of
drinking companions,' he continued, 'I tried to edge away.
But the old boy would have none of it.

' "Let's mull over old times, Bill," he said.

'He insisted we had lots of friends in common, which I'd
never heard of and were probably all dead anyway. So I
decided that the only plan was to humour him. With any
luck he'd either go to sleep or drop off the stool and break
his ruddy neck. But he'd just asked me how dear old
Romano's was doing when my clinical instincts came to
the fore. Remembering that such cases must be forced to
take a little solid protein occasionally, I said, "Don't you
think you ought to have a bite to eat?"

' "Eat?" He sounded as though I'd suggested we sent for a chess board.

' "Well—just a ham sandwich, or something."

' "Ham? Damn it, man!" he shouted. "Are you trying to kill me? The doctor's put me on a salt-free diet. George! Two more rum swizzles." '

'An unco-operative patient,' Nikki murmured.

'Exactly. I mentioned something about enough being enough, and the old boy started to become very excited. Knowing what would happen if I upset him, and not having a strait-jacket handy, I gave in. After all,' he explained, 'I have over the years developed a fair tolerance for the drug alcohol. I had a modest confidence that I could sit him out, particularly as he'd probably been at the rum swizzles since breakfast. So I joined him in another couple, while he told me he was the younger son of an earl and started singing *Abide With Me*.'

Grimsdyke started to take another drink of beer, but hesitated.

'It was then I began to feel some unusual symptoms myself,' he said.

'Simon,' he asked, after a pause. 'Do you remember that housemen's party we had in St Swithin's? The night we decided to fortify the fruit cup with a little absolute alcohol from the path. lab.?'

'I don't think any of us can possibly forget it,' I told him.

At the time our cellar in the Medical Officer's Quarters was reduced to a bottle of claret and a bag of oranges. To celebrate some fellow-resident's engagement Grimsdyke suggested making a claret cup of the type popular for young ladies' birthday parties, but adding some of the pure ethyl alcohol used to prepare microscope slides of bacteria.

'After all,' he had explained at the time. 'It's the methyl sort of alcohol that makes you end up as an interesting article in the *Lancet*. This is perfectly pure C_2H_5OH, exactly the same as you'd get from a bottle of champagne if you distilled it instead of drinking it.'

'But even ethyl alcohol's got to be treated with respect,' I had told him doubtfully.

'Exactly, my dear chap. People simply make the mistake of forgetting it's seventy-five over proof, and not adding it in judicious quantities. This is all going to be done highly scientifically. I'm going to scrounge a pipette from the biochemistry lab. and slip fifty millilitres into the mixture whenever the party shows signs of flagging. It'll be as precise as an intravenous infusion.'

This worked excellently until Grimsdyke had taken several glasses of the cup himself, when his impatience increased while his inhibitions diminished and he started tipping it from the Winchester quart hidden under the table. Some remarkable scenes had then ensued, and even when we'd cleared up all the foam we still didn't know where to bury the empty fire-extinguishers.

'My clinical state that evening at St Swithin's,' Grimsdyke continued at our hearthside, 'was exactly reproduced in the Savoy Hotel, Poparapetyl. I had vertigo and diplopia and my stomach felt as though someone had been at it with a bicycle pump. Even old George the barman woke up and looked worried—though probably only because we hadn't paid for the drinks. Anyway, he helped me off my stool and into a bedroom next door, while the old boy was deep in conversation with a stuffed monkey. I collapsed on an old iron bedstead with one leg off, wishing I were nicely tucked up in St Swithin's with an ice-bag and lots of trained nurses.'

He stopped, seeming pale even at the recollection.

'Then you passed out?' Nikki asked sympathetically.

'Graduates of St Swithin's Hospital, madam, do not pass out. Remembering my ill-spent youth, I focused my eyes on a spot on the ceiling, which turned out to be a squashed cockroach. But at least it rallied the neurones for action. It became pretty obvious that I couldn't be found on my first day dead drunk in some shanty. It also became obvious that if I stayed there I should rapidly be consumed by *orthoptera*. So after a bit I took a deep breath, got up, grabbed my hat, and without looking right or left started up the road home, hoping I was going in the right direction.

'I shall never forget that walk. Going out it had seemed a fairly easy half mile, but now it was like crossing the Sahara. The only thing that kept me going was the thought of my cool white air-conditioned couch at the other end. I've heard a good bit about the evils of drink in my time, but it wasn't till then I realised what the chaps with the big drum at the street corner really meant. But at last I staggered into my bungalow, hoping to heaven no one had seen me, and collapsed on the counterpane.'

'But,' Grimsdyke went on sadly, 'a doctor's work is never done.'

'You mean you didn't even have time to sleep it off?' I asked.

'I suppose I must have dozed for a few moments, but suddenly there was a terrible knocking on the door. I got up, feeling like the Drunken Porter with Macduff on the mat. Outside I found the Poparapetylian turnkey I mentioned earlier, in a bit of a state.

' "Come quick, doctor, sir!" he said, grabbing my coat, "one of the bosses taken mighty sick, my word!" '

'Much worse than a Casualty call after a St Swithin's party,' I observed.

'It was like coming round from one of Tony Benskin's anaesthetics. But never have I shirked my professional duty, old lad. The brain was functioning pretty clearly, even though I did feel someone had replaced my spinal cord with calf's foot jelly. If the big noise from the office had chosen this moment to give in to his blood pressure, as the only doctor in sight I had to cope.

'While I trudged after the turnkey for miles, trying to remember the right treatment for hypertension, I made a big resolve—at the end of the month's job, Grimsdyke would be shipped back to the temperate climes. Even Monica Fairchild was preferable to massive necrosis of the liver.

'But at last we came to a halt.'

' "In here, Doctor, sir," the chap said. "Very bad case, Doctor." '

'I felt the scene looked vaguely familiar. Sure enough, here we were again at the Savoy Hotel. I thought my patient might be the old boy, but he was sitting in his place as usual and merely said, "Doctor? Why, it's old Jim Parsons from Harley Street, bless me. Can't have set eyes on you for years. Still looking after all those pretty actresses?"

'Then—can you imagine my feelings?—the turnkey showed me into the room which I had with such suffering just evacuated. George the barman must have hurried off, scared stiff, to find the doctor. And here I was—the only member of the profession who's ever been called out for a consultation on himself.'

'And I don't believe a word of it,' said Nikki. 'You're just having Simon on, to get your revenge for Lady Corrington.'

'Every word's true, on my Hippocratic oath,' Grimsdyke insisted. 'If you don't believe me, go out to Poparapetyl and find out.'

'Whatever happened, it's a very good thing you didn't stay there,' she decided.

'You can do quite enough damage to your liver during English licensing hours,' I added.

'*J'y suis, j'y reste*, anyway,' said Grimsdyke lightly. 'If it's all right with you, Nikki's kindly offered to put me up, as I can't get the Aussie out of my flat for a bit. Now if you'll excuse me, I'd better go and get my kit out of the car.'

As soon as Grimsdyke was out of earshot I gave Nikki a paraphrase of my conversation with Sir Lancelot.

'Jolly decent of the old chap, don't you think?' I said warmly. 'Even though scholarships and grants and so on have changed the scene even since we were medical students ourselves, it'll be no end of help having some of Sir Lancelot's cash in the till.'

'A thing like that needs an awful lot of thinking over,' said Nikki.

'Oh, come, darling! It's the sort of offer any man would jump at these days.'

'I think I'd very much rather bring our children up independently.'

'I know, dear, and so would everyone. But once we've got another mouth to educate——'

'And it would be simply terrible having a man like Sir Lancelot shaking his will at us for the rest of his life.'

'Well, perhaps so,' I told her awkwardly. 'But anyway, with Sir Lancelot it's almost impossible to refuse.'

She stared at me. 'Simon! You don't mean you accepted —just like that?'

'But how on earth could I do otherwise? It would have been easier for the Prodigal Son to announce that he didn't care much for veal.'

'Simon, really!' She sounded rather annoyed. 'You are sometimes the biggest——'

'Hello, hello!' exclaimed Grimsdyke, reappearing with his bag. 'Sorry to butt in. If you two want a family row I'll go out and water the geraniums.'

'We haven't quite started throwing the crockery yet,' Nikki told him, smiling.

'How long are you staying, Grim?' I asked, glad to drop the subject.

'About a fortnight, if that's agreeable.'

'Perfectly. If you don't mind sharing a bed with Sir Lancelot Spratt on Tuesday week.'

'I'm off on Monday night,' said Grimsdyke promptly.

Nikki gave a gasp.

'He's not actually coming *here*?'

'I'm afraid he didn't give me even half a chance to put him off. But don't worry, dear—honestly. He's not always like you saw him in your surgery finals. He's really a kind-hearted man. It's just that he hides his light under a bushel.'

'Yes, and the trouble is the bushel keeps bursting into flames,' said Grimsdyke.

'I suppose I must just try and rise to the occasion,' said Nikki anxiously. 'I can always keep my confidence up by remembering I'm doing about the only single thing in the world he can't.'

11

For the next few days our lives were dominated by preparations for Sir Lancelot's arrival much more than the baby's.

'I'll have to get some flowers and of course some guest towels and a special tray-cloth for his early-morning tea,' said Nikki over her shopping-list. 'I suppose he does have early-morning tea?'

'At seven-fifteen promptly,' I told her. 'And it must be *china* tea.'

'China tea,' she murmured, writing it down. 'I hope they've got some in the grocer's. I can fetch it when I collect the Bath Olivers and the Double Gloucester.'

'And whatever you do, you mustn't forget to put *The Times* on his tray. He likes to discuss the leaders over breakfast.'

'*Times* on tray,' repeated Nikki. 'Do you suppose he'll like our nice nylon sheets?'

'I don't think he will at all.'

'I'd better buy a pair of ordinary cotton ones, then. And what on earth shall I give him to eat?'

'He believes in doing himself pretty well, you know. He's had some terrible rows with the dietetic experts.'

'Perhaps a cold roast chicken would be safest?'

'And I'll get a bottle of decent hock. Also some whisky and soda—he always likes a night-cap. Major Marston hasn't left any of his cigars about, I suppose?'

'Talking of night-caps, shall I buy a hot-water bottle?'

'Most definitely. And a thermometer thing to test the temperature of his bathwater. He generally brings his own trouser-press.'

We could hardly have been more thorough if we'd been expecting the Prime Minister himself.

Nikki said little more about Sir Lancelot's proposition, for like all women she was more concerned making the house as spotless for him as his own operating table. As Major Marston seemed to have been camping out rather than living in the place before our arrival, there was a good deal of scrubbing and dusting for her to do with the assistance of our latest 'woman.' We had employed several of these since our marriage, all with varicose veins and obscure lumbar complaints which they described in loud voices over their buckets, before leaving abruptly through some unfathomable psychological disturbance.

As someone always seemed to want to clean the spot where I happened to be sitting, I generally went out and played golf with Grimsdyke. The rest of the time our guest mooched about the house telephoning compli-cated instructions to his bookmaker and reading the 'Vacancy' advertisements in the *British Medical Journal*.

'Not much this week,' he said, tossing the grey-covered paper aside on the following Sunday evening. 'I usually stick to the "Miscellaneous" lot at the end. Occasionally you run across something like "Prosperous drug manufacturers want personable young doctor to take visiting Americans out to lunch." But this week there's only a lot of chaps trying to flog their old microscopes and a warning not to send original copies of testimonials.'

'Something suitable for your peculiar talents is bound to turn up before long,' I told him consolingly. 'Who knows—they might be wanting a new M.O. at The Windmill.'

'I never really lose any sleep over being unemployed, old lad. It's the only chance I have to escape from this ghastly modern obsession about work. And thanks to the oil company, I've enough in the bank to keep body and soul apart a bit longer.'

He paused, sticking a cigarette in his holder thoughtfully.

'On the other hand, of course, one can't go on like this,' he said abruptly.

'But why not?'

'Why not?' He seemed for a few moments to be trying to find a reason. Then to my surprise he got up and started pacing about our sitting-room.

'Old lad,' he said suddenly. 'Have you noticed anything odd about me while I've been here?'

I looked at him carefully.

'You're wearing the new cut-away sort of collar.'

'No, no! Nothing like that. Something—well, fundamental, if you'll excuse the word.'

'I've thought you've been a bit moody. But I put that down to the after-effects of Poparapetyl and backing all the wrong horses.'

'You have been witnessing,' Grimsdyke declared quietly, 'a soul in travail.'

'Good Lord, have I really?' I glanced at him nervously. 'What on earth's been going on?'

He sat down for a moment in silence.

'As we're alone, I'll tell you. I'm going to get married.'

'You're going to get *what*?'

It was as though Romeo had announced in the middle of the balcony scene that he had to get back for his cup of Horlicks.

'Don't get excited, old lad,' he went on quickly. 'There's nothing drastic in view. I mean I'm going to get married in theory. The practical will come later.'

'Then I'm delighted to hear it,' I said.

I felt the gratification of any Englishman whose friend announces he'd like to put up for his club.

'But why this sudden melting of the heart?' I asked. 'A few months ago you sounded ready to enter a monastery, if you could only find one with central heating and a club licence.'

'It's Nature,' Grimsdyke said simply. 'I've been a beastly sort of chap——'

'Oh, come! Unappreciated in certain quarters, perhaps.'

'But I have. Mucking about with the affections of young women at the peak of their reproductive activity. But these last few days, enjoying the hospitality of your little home and watching Nikki turning out little white things, surrounded with all those baby's baths and what-not you've shoved upstairs——' He shrugged his shoulders. 'It's the old paternal instinct, I suppose.'

'It's nothing to be ashamed of.'

'Oh, I know. The psychological pundits are perfectly right, of course. It's always there, however much you try

D

and cover it up with a neat blue suit and few light-hearted remarks.'

He was so distracted he let ash fall on his new silk waistcoat.

'I don't suppose the Grimsdykes came over at the behest of the Conqueror—much more likely at the behest of their creditors,' he went on. 'But did you know I'm the last of the line? I agree the proper reaction to that is, "And a damn good thing, too." But it seems a pity that the breed, for all its imperfections, should be lost to public view for good. And the only thing I can do about it is having some offspring or getting a glass tank of preservative spirit and presenting myself to the Natural History Museum.'

'You'd better have a drink,' I said.

I felt the conversation was becoming rather a strain on both of us.

'The trouble is,' my friend went on, as I poured him some of Sir Lancelot's special whisky, 'that marriage mightn't suit me.'

'You might as well say that life mightn't suit you. Mostly, it's what you make of it.'

'But I can't run around in emotional short pants any more, that's obvious. That awful gaffe I made on the ship, not to mention the even worse one in the Arundel, wouldn't have happened if I'd known a bit more about feminine psychology than you can pick up in the back of a taxi. And I'm not getting any younger.'

He thrust his hands into his pockets despondently.

'When I looked into St Swithin's the other day it struck me how terribly young the sisters were getting. Significant, eh? Soon I'll have a crow's playground round my eyes, chins in cascades, and large areas of scalp exposed to the

stares of passers-by. And damn silly I'll look then with a
bunch of flowers trying to woo some sweet young thing of
twenty-one.'

'But with an address-book like yours, Grim, you could
get hitched up tomorrow if you wanted to.'

'Of course I know dozens and dozens of women,' he
agreed, not looking particularly enthusiastic at the suggestion. 'But . . . well, dash it, they're all very well
whooping it up in a night club at four in the morning, but
how would they do at tea and cakes with all my ruddy
aunts?'

'A very old problem,' I sympathised.

'I remember my old grandpa,' he continued reminis-
cently. 'The one who was eaten by a tiger at eighty-four.
"Gaston, my boy," he used to tell me, "never go to bed
with a woman you can't face over breakfast." I suppose
the old boy was right, though I'll bet the Mint to the
parish poor-box he never took his own advice.'

'But the world's full of girls to face over breakfast,' I
consoled him.

'Yes, and their families make damn sure to keep them
away from chaps like me. And if I don't find the right one
pretty soon, I'll be shackled for life to one of the other
harpies. Half of them seem to consider themselves the
future Mrs Grimsdyke already. They simply misconstrue
my customary affability, like poor Nanki-Poo in *The
Mikado*. Do you know, I've only got to ask a woman if she
likes fried eggs and she starts stroking my lapels and
purring wouldn't it be nice if she could fry mine. I ask
you!'

'Then if you really want some fatherly advice,' I said,
as he distractedly helped himself to more whisky, 'I'd tear

up your address-book and start from scratch. Though for God's sake don't hurry—that's fatal.'

He stared thoughtfully at his glass. 'Could you give me some sort of idea of—well, a suitable type?'

'My dear chap! It's far more dangerous to advise a man on his choice of wife than his choice of doctor. You get blamed if either turns out to be a dud.'

'I must find someone intelligent enough to talk to——'

'Who won't be too intelligent to talk to you.'

'I hadn't thought of that.' He flicked the ash off his cigarette gloomily. 'I don't really suppose I shall ever discover a suitable mate.'

'Of course you will, you idiot! You're a member of a highly respectable, not to mention highly marriageable, profession. Any family would welcome you into their bosom, once you get over the habit of eyeing every female you're introduced to as though you wanted to eat her.'

'Then I'll start looking tomorrow,' he said, cheering a little. 'Thank you, Simon, for your valued advice. Do you remember what old Sir Lancelot used to tell us as students? "For success in surgery, gentlemen, like success in everything else, you need three things—brains, beauty, and cash. If you've got one of 'em, marry the other two." Who knows? I might find all three in the same pair of nylons.'

'And even if you don't, you'll have a lot of fun looking for her,' I laughed.

Our profound conversation was then interrupted by Nikki coming in with a bucket to scrub the carpet.

12

THE moment of Sir Lancelot's arrival approached with the speed of an appointment at the dentist's.

The china tea and crumpets were in the larder, the hot-water bottle and thermometer hung in the bathroom, the chicken chilled in the deep-freeze, and the hock cooled in the cellar. There was nothing to do but await our guest with the same feelings of hopeful inadequacy as Passepartout waiting for Phineas Fogg.

'I'm clearing off now,' said Grimsdyke at breakfast the morning before. 'He might make a mistake in the day. I never was much of a one for taking risks.'

'You can always come back when the den's empty,' I invited him. 'I'd hate to think of you wandering about with no place to hang your fourteen suits.'

'Oh, I'll doss down in the Y.M.C.A., or anywhere I can get a bit of peace and quiet to write next week's article for the papers. Come to think of it,' he added with a grin, 'now I've got a bit of spare cash I've half a mind to take a room for the night at the Arundel.'

Grimsdyke shortly roared away in his Richard Hannay Bentley, presumably to search for lodgings and a wife.

Having a few minutes to spare before leaving for the

surgery, I mentioned Sir Lancelot's offer to Nikki—almost for the first time since my return from London.

'I know you think me awfully stupid and stubborn, Simon,' she said. 'And I suppose I am. But the whole idea seems to me quite wrong. It isn't even that he's one of your relatives.'

'I know exactly how you feel,' I told her patiently. 'But surely we shouldn't look a gift horse in the mouth? Particularly when it's got so many gold teeth. Don't forget we're the depressed middle-classes, crushed between the upper and nether millstones, or whatever it is.'

'I still don't think we should have anything whatever to do with it.'

'The old boy's got bags of oof, if that's what you're worrying about. He made it when you didn't have to hand it straight to the Government, and surgeons weren't so keen to settle for a suite of Chippendale or a dozen whisky for services rendered.'

'I'm not going to have any child of ours dominated by Sir Lancelot,' declared Nikki firmly. 'He may live yet for years and years——'

I agreed. 'Knowing him, he's got arteries made of indiarubber.'

'And I can just see him sitting there telling us how to bring them up. It wouldn't be fair on them. And it would be absolutely impossible for us.'

'But he isn't such a bad chap,' I insisted. 'And really a very humble one. He just puts on that manner like his operating clothes. Over the years both have become part of him.'

'Anyway, I don't agree with it,' said Nikki.

I knew that my wife could be rather strong-minded, this

having produced several beneficial effects on me since marriage, from keeping me out of the pubs to making me suspend my trousers with braces instead of a handy length of two-inch bandage. But I thought that, like all women, she was being unreasonable, and I said so.

'I'm not being unreasonable a bit,' Nikki returned. 'I suppose you'd say Eve was being unreasonable, if she'd stamped on the serpent.'

'Darling, we mustn't have anything as stupid as this upsetting us,' I pleaded. 'When most couples quarrel it's over lack of cash, not a surfeit of it. Let's not argue about it any more.'

But we did, of course, almost until Sir Lancelot's Rolls appeared in our road and to an invisible guard of honour behind the neighbours' curtains drew up at the front door.

I prepared myself to entertain my godfather in my own home with understandable nervousness. As a junior medical student at St Swithin's I had been secretly proud, over-awed, and hopeful of the connexion between us, but it had become clear at our first meeting in his operating theatre that Sir Lancelot himself made no allowances for the relationship.

'You, boy!' he had roared. 'You latest viper in my well-bitten bosom—what's yer name?'

'Why, I'm Simon Sparrow, sir,' I said smiling behind my surgical mask.

'Good God, are you? I thought you were Argyll-Robertson.'

To my mystification everyone in the theatre broke into a roar of laughter.

'Come over here and get your hands dirty,' commanded

Sir Lancelot, those parts of me visible between sterile cap and mask turning bright pink.

By the time I reached my lodgings that night my godfather had left me with the suspicion that I was not, after all, born to be a famous surgeon. This was confirmed a few months later when I was studying diseases of the eye, and discovered in a textbook of ophthalmology that 'Argyll-Robertson' described 'a small irregular pupil that reacts sluggishly.' For the rest of the course he treated me with exceptional and unrelenting ferocity, just to prove that he dealt with all students equally.

I now opened the door of his car.

'So this is your home?' demanded Sir Lancelot at once, stepping out. 'Stucco and solid comfort. Admirable.'

'My wife, sir,' I said.

Nikki approached down the path, looking as if she expected him to exclaim, 'Fe fi fo fum!'

'Enchanted,' said Sir Lancelot. He bowed gallantly. 'Didn't I examine you in your surgery finals?'

'Yes, you did,' said Nikki, with an anxious glance.

'There you are, Sparrow. I never forget a candidate. And I dare say, young lady, you *still* don't know the three things you'd advise an elderly colonel with an enlarged prostate to avoid?'

Nikki shook her head.

'Drinking stout, riding a horse, and reading the *New Statesman and Nation*,' said my godfather briefly. 'Let us go indoors.'

To my relief, he seemed to be in the mood of a jovial uncle up for the Derby.

Sir Lancelot immediately marched through the ground floor, examining our surroundings.

'Excellent, excellent,' he declared in the kitchen. 'I agree with all these modern gadgets. I'm not half such an old-fashioned stick-in-the-mud as everyone makes out, my dear,' he added to Nikki. 'And after all, half the secret of successful surgery is making things easy for yourself. Eh, Sparrow?'

'Oh, of course, sir.'

'Television, eh?' He frowned as he entered the sitting-room. 'The destroyer of conversation, cerebration, and ocular accommodation. Don't approve. Don't approve at all. However, as it will doubtless shortly be made com-pulsory for the entire population, there's nothing we can do about it except submit quietly to disuse atrophy of the grey cells.'

He inspected one of the Marston's chairs.

'Furniture modern, but well designed. Sloppy furniture's the cause of half your backaches, which we never had when we all sat on planks as God meant us to. There's nothing like upholstery for playing hell with your pelvis. How d'you heat the place?'

'Central heating, sir,' I told him. 'Boiler in the basement.'

'I approve of that, too. Why on earth the inhabitants of this country should persist in poisoning each other through their chimney-pots is totally beyond me. Rooms upstairs?'

'Four, sir. Two baths.'

'H'm. Well, Sparrow—your father told me you were doing well enough to buy and furnish your own house, but I must admit frankly I hadn't any idea you were doing quite so well as this. Congratulations.'

Nikki and I exchanged a glance.

'Well, you see, sir,' I began hesitantly. 'It isn't quite as simple——'

'There was once a time, I don't mind telling you, when I didn't think you had the brains to support a bowl of goldfish, let alone a wife. I can only say that I'm both thankful and honestly delighted I was mistaken.'

'Perhaps I ought to explain, sir——'

'Explain?' He frowned. 'Explain what?'

My courage failed me.

'Oh, nothing, sir.'

'How about a cup of tea? I'm famished.'

'Yes, at once, sir. Just have a chair, sir.'

I stared hard at Nikki. She seemed to agree that it was simpler to leave things as they were.

'I'll take your things to your room,' I went on quickly.

'Thank you, Sparrow. And kindly remove the brown-paper parcel from the larger suitcase.'

I struggled upstairs with his pair of heavy leather cases, and came down holding a large parcel tied with surgeon's knots.

'I must apologise that I never sent you anything for your wedding,' Sir Lancelot continued as we sat down at the tea table. 'As a matter of fact, I completely forgot the date. I was somewhat distracted over that St Swithin's business at the time, you understand. I am glad now to be able to rectify the fault in much pleasanter circumstances.'

I opened the package while he spread his first crumpet. It contained a silver affair with a couple of small spirit lamps underneath, that looked the cross between a samovar and a portable steriliser.

'It's very, very beautiful,' said Nikki, who is quicker at such things than me.

'I am delighted you think so, my dear.'

'It's really most kind of you, sir. I'm sure it'll look absolutely wonderful in the . . . in the . . . '

'Just regard it as an expression of my good wishes,' said my godfather airily. 'Now young lady,' he went on, to my relief turning his attention to my wife. 'I should like a little chat with you. You trained at the City General, I believe?'

'Yes, I did. Under Mr Diff.'

'Know the feller well. Always makes his nephrectomy incisions too low. I will confess that I myself at first opposed admitting women students to St Swithin's, largely because I felt there ought to be some entirely masculine preserve left in London outside Wormwood Scrubs. I imagined that in no time the medical school would be full of powder boxes and furbelows and babies in prams. But I was wrong, and I admit it,' he continued frankly. 'Most of the women turned out a damn sight better students than the men, not to say rather cleaner and better dressed. Do you know,' he went on to me, 'on one of my last ward rounds a feller actually turned up at St Swithin's in a *tweed jacket*. And when I enquired if he wished to be directed to the golf course he had the impudence to reply that he'd come to learn medicine, not *haut couture*. The students aren't what they were, and I'll maintain that against anyone.'

My godfather sat looking regretful for the days when a single glance from himself could make a young man feel instantly hanged, drawn and quartered on the spot.

'But times ever change, I suppose. These days I'm as out of date as a jar of leeches——'

'Surely not, Sir Lancelot,' interrupted Nikki politely.

'But I am,' he argued. 'I'm a general surgeon, like Ambroise Paré and Lord Lister. I was taught to tackle

anything from a brain to a bunion and from paronychia
to pancreatitis. Which is distinctly *passé* these days there's
a surgical specialist to match every organ.'

I knew that he was proud of his professional versatility,
which he had exhibited even in his last week at St
Swithin's by insisting on removing a pair of tonsils.
(Though the demonstration was not wholly a success, the
throat specialist summoned when the patient showed
no signs of recovery writing as his opinion, 'I advise
tonsillectomy.')

'Look at this National Health business,' Sir Lancelot
went on, the last crumpet disappearing. 'Not that I
disapprove of it. I don't disapprove of anything that
makes people call the doctor before it's time to call the
clergyman. I only object that we doctors know more about
human beings than all the politicos in Whitehall. But it
had to come, I suppose. They can't bribe the voters with
beer any more, so they have to bribe 'em with bromides
instead. What's for dinner?'

'Chicken mayonnaise,' said Nikki.

I was delighted to discover that my wife was becoming
rapidly softened towards Sir Lancelot, who—when he
wished—had a manner which could not only charm birds
from the trees but organs from reluctant patients.

'And a bottle of Niersteiner 'fifty-two,' I added.

'Capital! Remarkable, isn't it Sparrow,' Sir Lancelot
went on amiably, 'how food similes have dropped out of
fashion in medicine? I remember when we used to talk
frequently of prune-juice sputum or anchovy-sauce sputum,
or port-wine urine and coffee-grounds vomit. Now everything's tested chemically and measured in millilitres——'

'Just one moment, sir,' I said, getting up.

For some minutes I had been aware of our sitting-room becoming prematurely dark. I was lamenting the storm overclouding a pleasant late August afternoon, when I noticed a large van obstructing the front window. Opening the front door with curiosity, I found four men in white aprons on the mat.

'Number sixteen, Alderman's Drive?' asked the leader.

'Yes, that's right. But I haven't ordered anything.'

'We've come for the stuff.'

'Stuff? What stuff?'

'Why, all the stuff, of course.'

'I don't quite understand——'

'The stuff from the house.'

With feelings perhaps resembling Grimsdyke's in the Savoy Hotel at Poparapetyl, I noticed that the side of the van announced HAMBLE & GRIMLEY SPEEDY REMOVERS.

'Surely there's some mistake?' I argued.

'Doesn't look like any mistake here, Guv'nor. See what it says on the paper—"Remove furniture to store from residence four o'clock Tuesday order of Mrs Marston." Couldn't have it plainer than that, could you?'

'But it's nothing whatever to do with Mrs Marston!'

'Them's our instructions, Guv'nor.' The man turned to his companions. 'Right you are, lads. Let's get weaving.'

The four of them started to move in.

'Now look here! Just one minute——'

'Come off it, Guv. We've got our job to do.'

'But damnation! Can't you show a bit of common sense?'

'Common sense? 'Oo's showing any common sense around 'ere, I'd like to know?'

We had a brief but urgent argument on the doormat,

terminated by the arrival of an open scarlet Jaguar which roared up with Mrs Marston herself.

'Who are these people?' she demanded at once, glaring at me. 'Why, it's the doctor,' she exclaimed. 'That dirty dog hasn't gone and cut his throat, has he? If he has, let the little tyke bleed to death. You can take it from me, he isn't worth the saving.'

'Just one moment, Mrs Marston,' I said nervously. 'I'm afraid there's been something of a mix-up.'

'I'll say there has!' She threw back her bright red hair. 'Mix-up, indeed! And if I once get my hands on him I'll have him so mixed up he won't be fit for anything except the Chamber of Horrors at Madame Tussaud's, where he ought to have been years ago. Right you are, men,' she added to the removers, now standing uncomfortably twirling their caps. 'Do your stuff.'

'But one minute!' I tried desperately to shut the door. 'I—I've got guests inside.'

'Guests? What on earth are you doing entertaining guests here?'

'I—I rented the house. Furnished. By the year.'

'You certainly did nothing of the sort!'

'But I did,' I insisted. 'The other day. From your—er, Major Marston.'

'Har!' She sounded like Monica Fairchild, as Goneril. 'From that rat? It's not his house—it's mine, and every stick and scrap inside it. So's the money in his business if it comes to that, which I'm going to squeeze out of the vermin, penny by penny, in the Bankruptcy Court. Carrying on with that little mouse-faced secretary of his, who everyone knows has been in bed with half the Town Council——'

'Please, please! Don't turn us out just at this moment!' I begged. 'Won't tomorrow do? I'll buy the place if you like,' I added frantically. 'Furniture and fittings and all.'

'I wouldn't be at all surprised if you weren't hand-in-glove with the nasty piece of garbage yourself,' snapped Mrs Marston, becoming angrier. 'And if you imagine for one moment you can buy me off——'

'What the devil's all this row about?' demanded my godfather, appearing at my elbow.

'And who might *this* happen to be?'

'This happens to be, madam,' said Sir Lancelot, instantly drawing himself up, 'Sir Lancelot Spratt.'

'Well, keep your great big bearded face out of it,' said Mrs Marston.

Sir Lancelot gasped. I don't think his expression had been seen on earth since the stone hit Goliath.

'If these people stand in your way,' Mrs Marston commanded the removers, 'I'll send for a policeman.'

'Right you are, missus,' said the foreman, and started moving out the hall table.

'Has everyone gone totally insane?' demanded Sir Lancelot as soon as he could speak. 'Or is this your idea of a practical joke? What the devil's this rude person doing in your house?'

'You took the words right out of my mouth,' said Mrs Marston. 'Don't pack the silver, you men, until I've counted it.'

'Sparrow!'

A lifetime of ordering people about half-covered by a surgical mask had given my godfather the ability to gesticulate fiercely with his eyebrows.

'You will kindly explain instantly.'

'Well, you see, this isn't really our house, sir,' I told him, hardly aware of my own words. 'I rented it, sir. But I'm afraid I didn't rent it from the landlord, if you follow me. I suppose this lady is perfectly entitled to take all the furniture, sir. But it'll be quite all right for you to stay the night,' I went on quickly, catching sight of the bundle of sticks and canvas propped behind the front door. 'You can have my camp-bed.'

'You expect *me* to sleep on *that*? Good God, man! Fetch my cases. Fetch them at once. This very instant. I refuse to stand here to be insulted for one more second. You will find me in the car.'

'That's solved our problem about Sir Lancelot's money, anyway,' I said to Nikki some time later.

We were sitting in the carpetless and curtainless rooms that Mrs Marston, in deference to my wife's condition, had finally allowed us to occupy for the night.

'I wish it hadn't happened like this, though,' said Nikki miserably.

I put my arms round her and smiled. Now it was all over I felt a peculiar sense of relief.

'Nikki, my sweet, I know it all looks a bit disastrous at the moment. But if nothing worse happens in all our married life, we'll still be one of the world's luckiest couples, won't we?' I kissed her. 'And they didn't take the fridge?'

She shook her head.

'Then we've still got our dinner—cold roast chicken and 'fifty-two hock. Come on, darling—we can eat it on the kitchen window-sill.'

13

'My dear Mrs Marston——' I began.

'Call me Diane, dear, do.'

'My dear Diane, we are completely in your hands. I'm afraid we've simply got nowhere to go, except your house.'

It was a morning more than a fortnight later when Mrs Marston and I met again. Our rendezvous was a small hotel in South Kensington, which seemed to exist largely for the convenience of old ladies, parsons, and men of faded military appearance. We were sitting together in a small dark lounge, thickly forested with ferns which looked as weary of their surroundings as the residents.

'I'm sorry I made such a bloody little fool of myself the other afternoon,' she apologised briefly. 'It's that terrible temper of mine. And I was as strung up as hell. *You* know.'

'Perhaps it was a rather inconvenient moment,' I murmured meekly, calculating the chances of keeping a roof over the head of my wife and unborn child.

'And now your lawyer's told my lawyer the *lot*. And am I delighted! Do you know why?'

I shook my head.

'I'll tell you what I'm going to do the moment I lay

hands on that senile delinquent of a husband of mine. I'm
going to take him by the scruff of his dirty neck and drag
him straight down to Scotland Yard and tell them to
charge him with embezzlement, or whatever it is. Then
I'm going to put on my best hat and sit in the front row at
the Old Bailey, and after that I'm going down to Dartmoor
to watch him breaking stones for the next fifteen years,
which he's deserved ever since he got out of the cradle.'

She paused, coiling her indignation for another spring.

Our meeting had been arranged by Mr Robbinson, my
family solicitor, a thin bird-like man rustling in a nest of
red-taped papers high above Chancery Lane, whom I had
known since the days when he would playfully tickle my
ears with a writ.

'You have been a very foolish young man,' he had told
me severely, when I called at his office earlier in the
morning.

I agreed with him. I had a pregnant wife, no home, little
furniture, an infuriated godfather, and—worst of all—the
self-humiliation of people who have bought gold bricks,
shares in imaginary oil-wells, Tower Bridge, and other
tempting bargains.

'Surely you of all people must know the danger of
scorning professional advice?' Mr Robbinson continued.
'The result may perhaps not be quite so disastrous in law
as in medicine, but I assure you that it is generally equally
uncomfortable for the patient.'

He drew a slip of paper from a desk piled with the hopes
of a score of litigants.

'I have been making a few enquiries about Marston,' he
went on in a gloomy undertone to his top waistcoat
button, the confidant of all his conversations. 'The man

has absconded to Australia—an enterprising part of the world, with the added attraction of being beyond the jurisdiction of the British courts. He is in company with the co-respondent, upon whom he has no doubt lavished your quarter's rent. You will, of course, never see your money again. If it is any consolation to you, neither will a lot of other people.'

'I'm afraid it isn't much consolation,' I murmured sadly.

'Meanwhile,' Mr Robbinson declared with some professional satisfaction, 'you and your wife are liable to be evicted from the premises forthwith. And you can naturally be sued for trespass into the bargain. Why, you haven't even got a tenancy agreement.'

'I'm certainly going to get everything signed on the dotted line in future, believe me.'

'Mrs Marston seemed on the telephone a somewhat volatile young person. But as there is no doubt about her *bona fides* I can only suggest you make yourself as agreeable as possible to her, in the hope she may let you remain *in situ*. Possibly,' he concluded, 'your profession will be of more use in the circumstances than mine.'

I found it difficult to make any impression at all on the wronged Mrs Marston, as she spent the first half an hour talking incessantly about her husband. Nothing is more boring than stories of other people's marital adventures, though I had to hear so many in my professional hours I could have patiently endured another; but unfortunately she used a voice that brought several old ladies peering through the ferns like startled animals in the jungle, and scowls from a faded military man reading the *Telegraph* opposite.

'And what do you think of *that* for the conduct of a so-called gentleman?' she ended some involved episode centring round a hairbrush.

'I think you've been a very brave woman,' I said, this being my stock and prudently non-committal reply.

She paused to use her lipstick.

'As I mentioned,' I went on anxiously. 'I'm afraid we've nowhere to go. We've a bit of furniture of our own——'

'Sorry I had to take mine, dear. I've got a flat in the Earls Court Road, and I'm simply lost without the telly.'

'And particularly in view of my wife's condition——'

She gave a laugh.

'I was forgetting about that. Poor duck! It must be terribly dull for you.'

'No, it's rather interesting, as a matter of fact.'

'Who are you having a flirtation with?'

I looked rather surprised, but admitted, 'Not with anyone, I'm afraid.'

'Aren't you really? But men have the most tremendous flirtations when their wives are expecting. All the ones I know do—some of them with me.'

She gave me a smile as smooth as her nylons, and probably just as synthetic.

'Now, if we could arrange some sort of tenancy agreement——'

'Do you know the Earls Court Road, dear?'

'Not very well.'

She sighed deeply.

'It's terribly lonely being a woman all by herself in the world again. Without even a damn soul to tell your troubles to. Do you remember when I told you all my troubles once? It was the first time you looked at my chest.'

'Of course,' I replied, feeling such grateful memories should be encouraged. 'I hope I did you some good.'

She clutched my hand. 'You did me *the world* of good.'

'About a tenancy agreement——'

'Do you know what I'd like to be doing more than anything else at this very moment?'

'That is, if you'd let us go on living there——'

'I'd like to be lying tucked up in bed, with you beside me listening to all my troubles. Even the ones I never told that hog of a husband of mine, supposing he'd had the good manners to listen.'

'Disgusting!' exploded the man opposite, crumpling his *Telegraph* and stalking away.

'Now what on earth did he mean by that?' demanded Mrs Marston indignantly. 'Do you think he's being insulting?'

'Perhaps it was something he read in the paper,' I said quickly. 'About the agreement——'

'I'm not at all sure you shouldn't give him a punch on the nose. There's far too many people of his type about these days. I don't think I like this place anyway. Good God, is that the time? I've got to be at Kettner's in two minutes. Get me a taxi, dear.'

'Mrs Marston—Diane——' I implored, following her into the street determined to continue the conference at all costs. 'About your house——'

'There's a taxi. Taxi, taxi! *What* about my house?'

'Can we please stay in it?'

'Why, do you want to? I'm much too flustered to talk about things like that just now. Bye, bye dear. You go back and give that old so-and-so in the hotel a piece of your mind.'

'But the house——'

'Come and see me in the Earls Court Road. Any time. Just give me a ring.'

She shouted her telephone number from the cab and swept off, and for the first time I felt a twinge of sympathy for her husband.

'I seem to be completely useless at any sort of business negotiation,' I said hopelessly to Mr Robbinson on the telephone a few minutes later. 'Perhaps you'd better handle it all yourself.'

'She might be persuaded to sell the property,' he conjectured sombrely. 'Though that would be somewhat expensive for you. I might be able to arrange a mortgage, but you will still have to find a sizeable sum yourself.'

'Do whatever you like,' I said in desperation, and rang off.

I felt that Mr Robbinson would at least escape the invitation to the Earls Court Road.

I also felt that I was totally inadequate for the responsibility of conducting a wife and child through the world, but there seemed nothing else I could do. I moodily took a sandwich and a cup of coffee in a teashop and I went as usual to my Thursday clinic at St Swithin's.

Doctors have a weakness for escaping from the world into their profession, and as I pushed aside the heavy glass doors of the surgical block that afternoon, to sniff the familiar mixture of antiseptic, floor-polish, and stewing fish exhaled by all British hospitals, I had a warm feeling of homecoming. Englishmen show the same unaffected reverence towards their old tutorial establishments as Americans towards their old mothers, and I was unashamedly fond of the ancient place—though St Swithin's was not in fact thought particularly old among the stately hospitals of England which stand so inconveniently in the middle of our industrial towns. It was young compared with Guy's, which was founded on a successful speculator's profits from the South Sea Bubble, and infantile compared with St Thomas's, which rose on the banks of the Thames in company with the Tower. St Swithin's was said to have started as an apothecary's shop on the green northern edge of the City, once patronised by Dr Johnson seeking a cure for the melancholy, and evolved like such successful institutions as our Monarchy, Parliament, and Church by a series of brilliant makeshifts. Nourished by the purses of the City merchants it turned into an Almshouse for the Sick Poor, which under the Victorians became an Institution for the Industrious Indigent, and under the National Health Service an adjunct to North Metropolitan (No. 15 Area) Regional Hospital Board. Meanwhile its buildings struggled like trapped animals to regain the countryside which yearly receded further, until in the middle of the nineteenth century they gave up the fight and came to rest between two sets of railway lines and a gin distillery, where today they present much the same appearance as first depressed the wounded veterans of the Crimea.

As stomach ache can be caused by anything from duodenal ulcers to unrequited love, the gastric clinic at St Swithin's was run jointly by Mr Hubert Cambridge, F.R.C.S., one of our surgeons, Dr. Peter Pennyworth, F.R.C.P., the senior physician, and Dr Granley-Dowkins, D.P.M., the psychiatrist. The patient's fate largely depended on which of this abdominal triumvirate laid hands on him first, Mr Cambridge giving his sufferers a cheerful slap on the umbilicus with the advice 'You'll be far better

off with it out,' Dr Pennyworth taking them into his ward
for six weeks on a bland diet, and Dr Granley-Dowkins
plunging into their subconscious sexual activity at the age
of two. Although some of Mr Cambridge's cases continued
to complain of their non-existent stomachs, and one of
Dr Granley-Dowkins' perforated his duodenal ulcer on the
analyst's couch, the clinic worked usefully and was even
applauded as an enlightened essay in social medicine. As
it is the job of the family doctor to explain away specialists'
failures for the rest of the patient's life, I was chosen to
attend as their representative—though perhaps less through
my clinical abilities than the personal friendship I had
enjoyed with Mr Cambridge over several years.

That afternoon I trod the well-known corridors warily.
I'd had no communication from my godfather beyond a
curt acknowledgment of my letter of apology, but I
thought it unlikely that his uncomfortable half-hour with
us would drive him straight back to Herefordshire. I had
heard of his old consulting desk being moved into his new
study, where he sat every morning staring across some of
the prettiest scenery in England struggling to start his
memoirs and finish his monograph *Spratt on the Colon*;
but I felt that the remote contemplation he had promised
both himself and his colleagues would be difficult.
Medicine is as gregarious an occupation as bus-conduct-
ing, and Sir Lancelot had reached the eminence at
St Swithin's of being unable to move about the place at
all without a sizeable procession immediately forming up
behind him. After a lifetime of being followed everywhere
by housemen, registrars, secretaries, sisters, students, and
anyone curious to discover what all the fuss was about, he
suddenly found himself with no one to impress but his

neighbours, no-one to command but his fruit pickers, and no one to talk to but Lady Spratt, who had rumbled him long ago. I felt that he might again be prowling round the hospital, with the same demoralising effect on the inhabitants as Jim Corbett's man-eaters prowling round Kumaon.

The gastric clinic was held in a long, cold, tiled room on the third floor of the out-patients' department, into which appetising smells from the kitchen were constantly wafted through the agency of some malevolent architect. The apartment was divided into sections by the familiar hospital screens, behind which I could hear as I entered the murmur of the three specialists pursuing their separate paths to eupepsia.

I had a battered consulting desk in one corner, with a rack of coloured forms and a big pewter inkpot which probably hadn't been used since consultants wrote their prescriptions with the care of Latin elegiacs. I slipped on a white coat as I bade good afternoon to our rather superior nurse, who must have been learning to drink her school milk through a straw when I first came to St Swithin's myself, and prepared for the problems of my first patient.

But I had hardly sat down when Mr Cambridge appeared.

'Ah, there you are, Simon,' he said at once. 'Been looking for you all round the refectory at lunch.'

'I found a bite outside,' I explained. 'I had an appointment at the other end of London.'

'Nurse, I think Dr Granley-Dowkins wants you.' He waited while she disobligingly wandered out of earshot and went on, 'Will you forgive me, my dear chap, if I ask you to discuss a personal matter?'

'Of course I will,' I said readily.

Mr Cambridge seemed unusually agitated. The most popular consultant at St Swithin's, he was an amiable, short, fat, pink man with half-moon glasses, a surgical Mr Pickwick, who was famous in the hospital for being rather absent-minded. Fortunately for his patients he never forgot an abdomen, but he was generally unable to recall where he was going, where he had come from, or whether he had had his lunch. The diaries which showered on him each Christmas being scattered all over London by Easter, he managed his daily life only by going from one activity to the next by a series of conditioned reflexes, like Pavlow's dogs. Perhaps he was the last of the medical eccentrics, who have unhappily been steadily dying out since the eighteenth-century surgeon John Sheldon insisted on embalming his dead mistress and keeping her in his bedroom until she was eventually ousted by his wife.

'Your godfather, Simon,' Mr Cambridge began, absently tearing up a test meal request form. 'Do you happen to know what brought him to London?'

'Oh, that's quite simple. Some family business about that child I told you we're having.'

'Good gracious, are you having a baby? I didn't even know you were married. But have you any idea,' he went on anxiously, 'how long he'll be staying?'

'He may have gone back already for all I know. Our business is concluded—quite concluded. I haven't any idea where he is.'

'I have,' said Mr Cambridge. 'He's staying with me.'

We passed a second of mutually sympathetic silence.

'I'm delighted, of course,' the surgeon continued. 'Absolutely delighted. He may be a rather difficult guest, but it's not often one gets the chance of inviting so dis-

tinguished a colleague to share one's home. Though I
didn't actually invite him, I suppose,' he reflected. 'He
just sort of arrived.'

'Has he been seen in the hospital?' I asked immediately.

'Seen? My dear chap, he's hardly ever out of the place.
Now he's no routine clinical work to occupy him, of course,
he's plenty of time for visiting us. Though it is sometimes a
little awkward, I must admit. Just when I'd got used to
him staying out of my operating theatre, too.'

Sir Lancelot had for several years the habit of dropping
into Mr Cambridge's theatre between his own cases,
making thin jokes over the surgeon's shoulder if he were
in a good mood, or staring in silence for ten minutes before
sniffing loudly and departing if he were in a bad one.

'Which reminds me,' Mr Cambridge went on. 'He
wants to see you tonight at half-past six, at my house.' He
paused as he caught my eye. 'Perhaps he would really
have been happier if he'd stayed among his fruit,' he
added. He gave a sigh. 'And perhaps we should have been,
too.'

14

THE clinic was a short one that afternoon. Afterwards Mr Cambridge hurried off to Harley Street to see those patients who had saved enough from their surtax to add to his own, while I telephoned Nikki before idling an hour or so in the medical school library and driving north to the Cambridge household in Finchley.

Mr Cambridge had the misfortune of being Sir Lancelot's particular professional protégé. In the days when my godfather was the red-bearded Mr Spratt, with a reputation already sweeping the corridors clean of students on his operating afternoons through the twin excellence of his professional instruction and his highly unprofessional anecdotes, he had spotted young Cambridge's surgical potentialities and secretly determined to train the lad himself. Mr Cambridge was personally planning to take his new degrees back to the bloodless peace of the University, to smoke donnish days away watching successive crops of geraniums and undergraduates mature in the college court, but the afternoon the examination results appeared Sir Lancelot had stopped him on the steps of the medical school.

'So you won the gold medal in surgery, eh, Cambridge?'
he asked abruptly. 'Don't look so modest about it, boy. I
only just managed it myself. What now?'

'I've put in for a fellowship at Trinity, sir,' Mr Cambridge told him nervously.

'Then withdraw it.'

'I—I beg your pardon, sir?'

'You heard what I said. You'd be no earthly good at
research, you can take it from me. And if I didn't know
my students' minds better than they do themselves I
wouldn't even teach needlework.'

'Then what shall I do instead, sir?' cried Mr Cambridge
in despair.

'Apply for my house-surgeon's post. You may think it
over and telephone me this evening. Not between eight
and nine, or you'll spoil my dinner.'

This invitation surprised Mr Cambridge greatly, particularly as Sir Lancelot had that morning hurled a blood-
soaked swab at his head with the remark that he was
'about as much use as a crate of corkscrews to the Band of
Hope.'

Sir Lancelot told Mr Cambridge every day for the next
year that he was the worst house-surgeon he had ever
suffered, then he promoted him and told him every day
for the next ten that he was the worst registrar he'd ever
suffered, too. It was the only way he knew to toughen such
a mild personality for the terrible self-criticism that runs
among the successes and failures of a surgical career;
but it left his pupil feeling afterwards like many other
middle-aged Englishmen when confronted with their
old headmasters.

I could see nothing of Sir Lancelot's Rolls as I now

drew up at Mr Cambridge's gate, but his own Bentley was already standing outside.

'Your godfather rang,' announced Mr Cambridge opening the front door himself. 'He's delayed. Perhaps you'd care for a glass of sherry in the meantime?'

As I made my way in I noticed a steamer trunk in the hall.

'Just arrived from Hereford,' explained Mr Cambridge quietly.

'I wonder what's holding Sir Lancelot up?' I asked. 'He's usually very punctual for appointments.'

'It's a committee meeting—the International Fraternity of Surgeons.'

'But he resigned from that!'

Mr Cambridge nodded. 'When he retired he resigned from everything—from the hospital rugger club to the Pantheon. Now he's written to all the secretaries withdrawing it, and no one seems inclined to disagree with him.'

'Of course, I'd be delighted if it means Sir Lancelot intends to spend more time in London,' my host continued, when he had fetched the decanter. 'I'm sure that all of us at St Swithin's would agree. It's only right that such great gifts as his shouldn't be lost to the hospital entirely. Though I must confess that he seemed rather surprised at the place continuing to function without him at all.'

My godfather's retirement had in fact given St Swithin's its greatest stimulus since the empty antiquated outpatients' block was blown up one night in 1941. Every consultant had been incubating little schemes to hatch in the milder climate once the thunder of his opinions had

rolled away, and Mr Cambridge himself had almost
at once started a statistical department (Sir Lancelot
declared statistics as unreliable as weather forecasts),
ordered air-conditioning for his operating theatre (Sir
Lancelot would as soon have ordered himself a bottle of
scent), and started smoking his pipe in the surgeons' room
(Sir Lancelot smoked only after dinner, and then only
Havannas).

'I'm honoured to offer him such hospitality as I can,'
the surgeon went on. 'Though of course it *is* a little difficult now I'm in the middle of all my plans for the bicentenary celebrations. You knew that Pennyworth got
the St Swithin's council to vote me to take charge?'

'Congratulations,' I said. 'Yes, I heard this afternoon.'

I had also heard of Sir Lancelot declaring publicly this
was only because Pennyworth put the motion at five
o'clock, when everyone was dying for their tea and would
have agreed to anything.

'I think I can get royalty to open the historical exhibition in the Founders' Hall,' he told me proudly. 'And
Mr McCurdie's statue to Humanity will look very well
inside the Main Gate. But for some reason your godfather
seems to object to—ah, hello, my dear,' he broke off, as
we were interrupted by his wife. 'Sir Lancelot rang to say
he'd be in for dinner as usual.'

'I'm sorry, Simon, that your godfather has become so
quickly bored with life as a country gentleman,' she said
to me.

'I think he rather misses the bustle of hospital life,' I
suggested.

I suddenly remembered that Celia Cambridge and Sir

Lancelot hated each other. For years they had conducted a complicated quarrel, the cause of which had long ago been forgotten by everybody including themselves, but which probably started when she kept him in control in the operating theatre by slapping freshly boiled instruments into his upturned thinly-gloved palm. Celia had been a famous theatre nurse at St Swithin's, and when Mr Cambridge proposed to her after a steamy courtship among the sterilisers all the other nurses who wanted to be catty—and there are always far too few marriageable young surgeons to go round—declared that if she managed her husband like she managed her theatre she'd have him in Harley Street in no time. She was barely tall enough to reach across an instrument trolley, but she had the determination of the Brigade of Guards.

'A pity he cut himself off so completely in the first place,' murmured Mr Cambridge, staring at the carpet.

'On the contrary, Bertie. I think it was a very good thing for the hospital that you got rid of him.'

'But he's a very great surgeon, my dear.'

'I'm not denying that for a moment. But if you'll excuse me for saying so, Simon, the way my husband and all the other men at St Swithin's let Sir Lancelot go on bullying them year in and year out is nothing short of a disgrace.'

'I was once his house-surgeon, my dear——'

'Which doesn't give him the excuse for treating you like one for the rest of your life.'

'My godfather *can* be rather difficult at times,' I admitted politely.

'*I* never found him difficult at all. Bertie refuses to stand up to him, and that's all there is to it.'

We heard the front door close.

'I'm going back to the kitchen,' said Mrs Cambridge promptly.

'Celia is a little overwrought to-day,' apologised her husband.

The sitting-room door opened, and Sir Lancelot was with us.

'Cambridge,' he said at once, ignoring me. 'I wish you to raise the question of the hospital telephones at the next meeting of the medical council. Must I always be answered by a casualty porter in need of attention by both the speech-therapy and child-guidance clinics? When I tried to get in touch with you this afternoon the man replied most impolitely to my entirely reasonable demands for efficiency, and then abandoned the instrument for fifteen minutes on the casualty reception desk. I was in this period informed by various people that my wife was as well as could be expected, I must drive my ambulance at once to King's Cross, and my stomach contents were ready if I would care to come and fetch them. Public relations, Cambridge! These days the telephonists are quite as important as the surgeons. I want to talk with you, Sparrow.'

'Yes, sir.'

'By the way, Cambridge, I shall be conducting a certain amount of personal business while I am here. It might be convenient for me to have the small room across the hall as my study.'

'Perfectly convenient, Lancelot.'

'What's for dinner?'

'I think Celia's got some . . . let me see . . . roast grouse.'

'Yes, I am fond of grouse. Now perhaps you will leave me for a few minutes with this young man.'

E

'My surprise at the scene I was obliged to participate in at your house,' Sir Lancelot went on when we were alone, 'was exceeded only by my amazement at reading your letter of explanation. To be taken in by a confidence trickster, and an amateur one at that, indicates a stage of mental retardation exploited by practitioners of the three-card trick on the corners of race-courses.'

'I'm very sorry about your inconvenience, sir,' I said humbly.

'And so you should be. It was only with difficulty that I found a bed for the night at the club.'

He paused, and went on reflectively, 'But one cannot live in a club for ever. One begins to suspect one is as decrepit as the other members look. It's a pity I sold the house in Harley Street. I never stay in hotels, of course. They kindly offered me a shakedown here,' he continued, looking round like a health visitor in some particularly unfortunate slum. 'Though it is not wholly satisfactory, and Cambridge's wife can sometimes be very irritating.'

'Do you expect to be staying long, sir?' I asked hesitantly.

'I must certainly stay a short while to give Cambridge a hand with the bicentenary. God knows what they're all up to at St Swithin's. Cambridge is of course perfectly hopeless on committees. He always loses his agenda and forgets to address the chair and votes the wrong way. Anyway, you can never hear yourself speak in the St Swithin's council for the scream of grinding axes.'

Doctors are enthusiastic politicians, and visitors to our big hospitals would be surprised to overhear the groups of specialists conversing earnestly in the corridors discussing not matters of life and death, but whether the building sub-committee could get away with painting the professor of bacteriology's new departmental lavatories bright pink.

'Committees are simply a means of providing our ruling classes with an excuse to waste time and a bit of excite-ment,' Sir Lancelot declared. 'A hundred years ago they had mistresses instead. Anyway, all the real work's done in the corridors outside. You might pour me a glass of that sherry.'

'What they really need to celebrate the bicentenary is a congress of the International Fraternity of Surgeons,' he announced as I handed him his drink. 'I shall have a word with Cambridge about it after dinner.' Then he asked abruptly, 'You still have a roof over your heads?'

'Strictly speaking, I'm afraid we haven't.'

'It is, of course, a matter of supreme indifference to me whether you yourself sleep in the nearest cowshed. It is only your wife who has my sincerest sympathy. You have tackled this hennaed harridan?'

'Mrs Marston? Not with much success, I'm afraid.'

'Why not?'

'She's rather difficult to handle, sir.'

'If you are incapable of handling difficult women at this stage of your professional career, I despair for you. I can only say—— Good God! What in the name of heaven is *that*?'

To my alarm he was staring in horror at something on the table behind me.

I was at first puzzled myself, turning round to discover an object resembling an ostrich egg with holes bored in it. But noticing the word 'Humanity' on a small pedestal underneath, I suggested, 'Perhaps it's the model for the new St Swithin's statue?'

Sir Lancelot flung open the door.

'Cambridge!'

'Yes, Lancelot?' Mr Cambridge appeared almost at once.

'Do you mean you actually intend to stick that inflated renal calculus on public view?'

Mr Cambridge followed Sir Lancelot's finger nervously. 'I'm afraid it has—er, already been commissioned from Mr McCurdie,' he admitted.

'Then tell the feller to knock up something different. If I ordered Humanity I'd expect to *get* Humanity. Something with angels and so on. Really, Cambridge! I must insist you get the council to countermand that pathological monstrosity at once. Yes, my dear?'

'Dinner is ready,' announced Mrs Cambridge, a little pale.

'Excellent! I am extremely hungry.' He turned to me. 'Would you care to stay for a bite?'

I explained that mine was waiting at home, and gratefully took the opportunity to say good-bye.

'I once learnt a very interesting way of preparing grouse,' I heard Sir Lancelot declaring as he made his way towards the dining-room. 'Which I shall demonstrate to you, my dear, one of these fine days.'

'Celia has asked me to say how delighted we are you're having a baby,' said Mr Cambridge, distractedly at the front door. 'Though—if you'll forgive me for saying so, Simon—it might have been very much easier for everybody if you'd put off the whole idea until after our bicentenary.'

15

' "*EITHER you or your husband must first have actually paid twenty-six contributions of any class for the period between the time of entering insurance and the date, or expected date, of your confinement,*" ' I read to Nikki.

' "*And second have paid or been credited (for example, for weeks of sickness or unemployment) with at least twenty-six contributions of any class for the last complete contribution year before the benefit year in which the confinement takes place, or in which the confinement is expected.*" Now what the devil does all that mean?'

I was studying leaflet N.I./17A, the sixteen-page pamphlet by which Her Majesty's Government instructs her subjects how to claim the compensations they have voted themselves for perpetuating the population.

'What on earth's the difference between a contribution year and a benefit year?' I grumbled.

I read on: ' "*A benefit year is a period of twelve months beginning five months after the end of the contribution year.*" What can they possibly mean by that?' I asked. 'It seems an awful pity for the chaps in Whitehall that God didn't decide on a tidy period of twelve months, with an extra day thrown in on leap years.'

'Nine months is *quite* enough,' said Nikki, putting down her knitting. 'Do you know what I'm going to do the moment I'm back in circulation?'

'Buy a lot of tight-waisted dresses?'

'I'm going to storm the platform at the next meeting of the Royal College of Obstetricians and insist on delivering a lecture. I'm going to call it "The Minor Disorders of Pregnancy," and announce it with a hollow laugh. For months I've had cramp, swollen ankles, varicose veins, heartburn, and backache—not to mention breathlessness and frequency—my face is puffy, my hair's ghastly, and I feel the size of the dome of St Paul's. And every time I complain to Ann she says what am I worrying about, my blood-pressure's fine, and looks at me as though I were being fussy.'

'Don't worry darling,' I told her cheerfully. 'It won't be for much longer. Pregnancy's an eminently self-limiting condition.'

'At the moment I'm getting terribly fed-up with the whole project.'

'A perfectly normal psychological reaction.'

Nikki snorted.

'Heaven knows what would happen if men could be pregnant. I daren't even begin to think of the fuss that would go on.'

My wife had burgeoned since the afternoon of Sir Lancelot's visit. The year had now reached that depressing season when dusk chases dawn so briskly across the English roof-tops, and the baby—which had previously seemed almost as theoretical as the drawings in my old embryology books—had a pulse of its own and was kicking like a Twickenham full-back. Its approach was signalled to the

neighbours by a string of washed new nappies fluttering
from the clothes line in the Marston's garden, for their
broken home was now our own. The negotiations had
been managed by Mr Robbinson, and I was frighteningly
in debt to something called the Everlasting Building
Society, whose directors seemed to take him a good deal
out to lunch. Nikki and I lived among a discarded suite
of my father's waiting-room furniture and several fretwork
bookcases made by her brother, but I was very content,
except when reading advertisements for fast cars. Meanwhile, Dr Ann Pheasant called frequently, poked Nikki's
abdomen like a jolly farmer befriending his pigs, and told
me the little nipper was lying beautifully and she thought
she could feel the feet.

My godfather, to my relief, now took little notice of us,
being far too occupied reorganising the plans for the St
Swithin's bicentenary. This interference disconcerted not
only Mr Cambridge but all the consultants in the hospital,
for though they all had agreed that the anniversary should
be celebrated they equally strongly all disagreed how. The
surgeons wanted to build more operating theatres and the
physicians more medical laboratories, the obstetricians
proposed a new ante-natal clinic and the pathologists a
new post-mortem room, the ophthalmologists suggested a
new ocular department in place of the disused laundry
(which they described as 'a perfect site for sore eyes'), the
hospital chaplain wished the event to be celebrated with
stained glass, and the director of the V.D. department
with a champagne party.

But Sir Lancelot championed none of these schemes.
There had been no more fearsome politician in the history
of St Swithin's, and his ability to breathe a word in the

right ear or to grasp the right lapel would in Westminster probably have put him in the Cabinet. Although no longer on the council himself, he persuaded sufficient old friends to vote for an International Surgeons' Conference and had already been heard booming to an advance party of Continental colleagues, '*Pardon mille fois que je suis en retard pour l'operation, messieurs, mais le big end de mon motor-car est allé au coin de Oxford Street.*' He was not a man to let anything so flimsy as a language barrier stand between himself and the personal expression of his opinions.

Sir Lancelot further disconcerted the St Swithin's staff by starting operative surgery again, by simply inviting himself to assist Mr Cambridge in his theatre. His notion of assisting at an operation was like the Yarmouth waiter's of assisting young David Copperfield with his dinner, and after declaring 'I want you to treat me exactly as yer houseman, Cambridge, and swear at me if I get in the way,' he would take over more and more of the procedure until he was shortly cutting out anything he fancied himself. Mr Cambridge meanwhile was becoming noticeably short-tempered and developing the beginnings of a facial tic.

'Is the old boy still staying with the Cambridges?' asked Grimsdyke, when Nikki and I met him in London a few days later.

'He's practically one of the family,' I told him.

'Poor old Cambridge!' said Grimsdyke.

'Poor Mrs Cambridge,' said Nikki.

We were enjoying what was probably my wife's final outing, sitting in the bar of a small West End restaurant where Grimsdyke had insisted on taking us in compensation for the dinner snatched from our lips at the Arundel. It was a plush-lined place with pink lighting which gave all the food the look of being laced with cochineal and all the guests of suffering from *polycythaemia rubra vera*, and the head waiter had given Nikki a look of fearsome disapproval on arrival; but Grimsdyke declared that it was the current place to watch all the fashionable actors, actresses, and politicians feeding themselves, if you wanted to.

'How about splitting a bottle of Bollinger before we eat?' asked Grimsdyke, turning to more serious topics.

As I hesitated, he added, 'Just the thing for Nikki's condition. All the old midder books advise a glass to keep the mother's spirits up, along with a daily ride in the Park. And don't worry about the bill,' he went on. 'Old McGlew's stomach is paying for it.'

'But hasn't he gone back to his pork butchery?' I asked in surprise.

'He's in town again. But having got fed up with the way they do boiled fish at the Arundel he's taken a tasteful flat in Grosvenor Square, where I continue to lavish medical attention on him. I don't want to boast, but the chap's come to rely on me so much I pretty well have to tell him when to change his socks. Besides,' Grimsdyke added, nodding towards the restaurant entrance. 'I've another guest arriving in a few minutes whom I particularly want to impress. What's your ogreish old godpop doing, anyway?' he demanded, ordering the champagne.

'Mainly wrecking all poor old Cambridge's plans for the bicentenary. Though why he should make such a nuisance of himself I don't know. Particularly when a few months ago he swore he wouldn't touch the business with the end of a long pair of forceps.'

'But haven't you heard the gossip?' asked Grimsdyke, who always had. 'Why, in order to mark the bicentenary of the dear old place,' he went on, as Nikki and I shook our heads, 'the powers that be are dishing out a knight-hood. You know, an honour for all worn by one, like when they give a medal to the captain of a ship which goes down very decently with all hands. It's all terribly secret, of course,' he added, lowering his voice slightly. 'And no one knows who's going to be the lucky chap. But obviously if old Cambridge runs the fun and games he's well in the running.'

'But why should a modest fellow like Cambridge let himself in for it in the first place?' I asked, feeling puzzled. 'I know he hates messing about with committees and he doesn't give a damn for titles. Anyway, his practice is big enough to do without a built-in advertisement.'

'Personally I can't imagine anyone wanting to be a knight,' Grimsdyke agreed, 'now that it doesn't involve something exciting in the line of rescuing beautiful maidens from dragons. You just have to make a lot of speeches and get touched by every charitable organisation in London. Though there must be something in it, I suppose,' he added inspecting the bubbles in his glass reflectively. 'Look at those chaps in the Civil Service, slaving away on a pittance—from ten to four, that is—just to call themselves Sir Thingummy Whatnot in Bournemouth for a couple of years before their arteries pack up.'

'For a surgeon who's reached the top,' I suggested, 'I suppose it's a way of going into posterity.'

'Either that or getting some ghastly disease named after you,' said Grimsdyke. 'I'll stick out for a barony myself. It must be jolly good fun getting up in the House of Lords and telling everyone what's wrong with the world, without even having to kiss a lot of beastly babies every five years.'

'I expect it's the wife who wants the title really,' said Nikki.

'You have a point,' Grimsdyke observed. 'They've said at St Swithin's for years that if she were dead and opened you'd find "Lady Cambridge" lying in her heart.'

Further speculation was interrupted by a waiter bending over my friend's shoulder and announcing, 'The lady has telephoned to say she will be a few minutes late, sir.'

'Thank you. I should shortly like you both,' he went on as we looked at him enquiringly, 'to meet the charming girl whom I hope will be the future Mrs Grimsdyke.'

'No!' Nikki and I exclaimed at once.

'Yes, indeed. You can't imagine the hours I've put in, Simon, since we had that little chat in your sitting-room last summer. Following your advice to the letter, the first thing I did on reaching Town was to cast my address book into the flames. As soon as it went up in smoke, of course, I knew I'd made a damn silly start—I could have flogged it for quite a bit of cash to the housemen at St Swithin's. But it was symbolic. A purified Grimsdyke was about to face the world.'

He looked at me, seeming disappointed that I did not appear particularly impressed. I was used to Grimsdyke's recurrent attacks of morality, when he would cut down his drinking, smoking, and betting, start out on a long walk, and even take his bath slightly cooler in the morning. The only difference over the present one lay in the spasm usually being precipitated by a severe hangover.

'Becoming a better man,' my friend went on, sipping his glass of champagne, 'has turned out to be a darned sight easier than finding the right girl. At first I was almost reduced to sticking a pin in the membership list of the

University Women's Club. Then I got the hang of it, and met some very decent females. If I might be allowed to say so, it's been a pretty close race that to-night enters the finishing straight. Did you remember that sweet little thing Angela Palgrove-Badderly?'

I frowned.

'The girl I was chatting to last week, the afternoon you were buying Christmas presents in Harrod's.'

'Ah, yes . . .'

'Of course, she only works in a shop because it's the fashionable thing among her friends. Angela's terribly aristocratic—they've got the old country house, or rather they did have until they let it go as a reform school. Presented at Court, too, or she would have been if they hadn't stopped the whole business. But the family's very modest about it all, and live in quite a little place near Holland Park. I got along with her famously. The only trouble was her father, a retired brigadier whom I think is suffering from some of those senile mental changes. Acted most oddly when I was there, sometimes.'

As Miss Palgrove-Badderly had seemed about sixteen and her conversation consisted in asking me if I knew a large number of people whom I didn't, I felt the attitude of her father was a stroke of luck. But Grimsdyke always did have a weakness for pretty girls behind counters.

'Then there was Hesta,' he went on, 'whom you never met. She really was intelligent. I don't think she could talk about anything that didn't affect the lives of half a million people. I ran into her in an espresso bar, and we saw quite a lot of each other for a while. I learnt all sorts of interesting things about state monopolies and the condition of the peasants in the Ukraine.'

'Pity you didn't marry her,' I remarked. 'You could have got through your evenings without television.'

'She wanted me to go to some sort of jamboree in Trafalgar Square, holding a placard,' he explained with a touch of embarrassment. 'I mean to say, there are limits to what a chap can do. On a Sunday morning, too, when I look forward to my little bit of lie-in. After that there was a nice girl called Amanda, who painted and kept falcons, but I won't bother you with all that. The fact is, the lady you are about to meet,' he ended, suddenly becoming solemn, 'is the one whom I feel fit to bear my children.'

'And I hope she enjoys it,' murmured Nikki.

'There's just one thing, old lad,' Grimsdyke went on anxiously. 'Having great trust in your judgement, I wonder if you'd just sort of . . . well, look her over critically before I commit myself to anything definite?'

'Really, Grim!' I exclaimed, 'you can't expect me——'

'Just for old time's sake,' he entreated. 'Remember at St Swithin's when you stopped me running off with that conjurer's assistant? I'll tell you what we'll do—we'll have a little code. If you think she's the horrors, say, "There's been a lot of rain for the time of year," and I'll take no further action. But if you think she's just the one, remark lightly, "It looks like a change in the weather," and I'll turn on the charm. How's that?'

'I'm sorry,' I said firmly. 'But if you're really contemplating such a serious step as marriage, the whole idea's completely out of——'

At that moment the waiter reappeared to announce, 'The lady has now arrived, sir,' and Grimsdyke made for the lobby.

'Surely you're not going to fall in with such a crazy scheme, Simon?' asked Nikki at once.

'Not on your life! That sort of thing was all very well when we were a couple of students messing about at St Swithin's, but I sometimes wish that old Grim would grow out of his delayed adolescence before it starts being taken for premature senility.'

'I wonder what she's going to look like?' said Nikki, glancing at the door.

'Oh, pretty smashing, I should think. He always could pick 'em, even as a penniless medical student.'

We were interrupted by the appearance of a handsome blonde girl about six feet tall, whom Grimsdyke led in as though she had just won the Derby.

'The Countess Suschika,' he announced proudly. 'From Latvia.'

16

HowevER ridiculous I thought Grimsdyke's code, we had hardly sat down to dinner before it was clear the ordinary obligations of friendship would compel me to use it. The Countess was far too strong a prescription for Grimsdyke's suffering celibacy.

'Have you left Latvia long?' asked Nikki to open the conversation, as the Countess started munching her way through a pile of *hors d'oeuvres*.

'Ach, no! I am not in Latvia since I am a tiny baby,' she explained. 'I am in Sweden and in Norway and in Germany, and now I am in Finland, where I learn the massage. And next I start a school of massage in London.'

'Lulu's a Scandinavian masseuse,' announced Grimsdyke proudly. 'As a matter of fact, we met over old McGlew's quadratus lumborum.'

'I do hope you'll like it in England,' I told her.

'Ach, yes,' she said warmly. 'You have such lovely things here. Such roast beef and bacon and eggs. And such fish and chips! They are so quaint, but I love them so much already.'

Grimsdyke caught my eye. 'Massaging people all day does rather take it out of you.'

'And what a lovely restaurant this is! It is much better even than the *Teatergrillen* in Stockholm. I do not care much for drink, which upsets my liver and my kidneys,' she said draining her wineglass. 'But eat I always can.'

The Countess got through her food with the fascinating efficiency of the garbage-disposal machine in our kitchen sink. She managed to talk a good deal at the same time, emphasising points of conversation by clasping Grimsdyke's wrist with hands which would have been the envy of a professional goalkeeper. But to my horror my friend seemed to regard all these only as fascinating little failings.

'And you, my dear,' Lulu said to Nikki, pausing to pick her teeth between courses. 'You do the exercises for expectant women, no?'

'Not very regularly,' Nikki confessed. 'So many of them seem devised for pregnant female contortionists.'

'I have a wonderful exercise for pregnant women,' declared Lulu, demonstrating with her arms. 'It is quite simple, you lie down and imagine you are breaking a plank with your knees. So good for the pelvis—and the woman's pelvis, my dear, is the most important thing in the whole world, is it not? It houses the human race. But you must have the massage. I shall give it to you. I give it to Gaston every morning.'

Grimsdyke looked rather shamefaced at this revelation, but murmured, 'Jolly useful for toning you up.'

'Why do you all muffle your bodies up so in England?' Lulu went on loudly. 'Is the body not a beautiful thing? You are doctors, you will agree. In Scandinavia we think it is very beautiful indeed. You would no longer cough and spit in each other's faces all winter if your bobbies let you walk about Hyde Park all naked.'

She paused as the next course arrived. I prepared to give Grimsdyke my frank opinion of his prospective bride.

'I hope you will soon have a change in this rainy weather,' said Lulu, just at that moment.

This put me in some confusion. I could only murmur feebly, 'The damp can't last much longer.'

'Do you mean there's been a lot of rain for the time of the year, Simon?' asked Grimsdyke pointedly. 'Or do you think it looks like a change in the weather?'

'I think myself it is going to freeze and snow,' said Lulu.

'I mean,' I said, trying to remember how our arrangement went. 'That we're in for a moist spell.'

'Now what on earth *do* you mean?' asked Grimsdyke, rather shortly.

'I told you perfectly plainly,' I replied, annoyed at being drawn into the performance at all. 'I said it's going to be wet.'

'Do you wish to state,' he continued, leaning across the table and speaking as though I were a difficult patient in the children's clinic. 'That there has been a lot of rain for the time of year? Or do you mean that it looks like a change in the weather? You must mean one or the other. I do wish you'd try and make up your mind which.'

'You can't blame me for hardly knowing what I mean,' I replied, feeling my face redden. 'The whole business is so confusing, not to mention being perfectly stupid.'

'Simon,' murmured Nikki.

'You English!' said Lulu cheerfully. 'Always arguing about the weather.'

She started about her pelvis again, but Grimsdyke skilfully switched the conversation to cricket.

'But surely he could never seriously have intended to marry *that*,' I said to Nikki, as we drove away later. 'Why, it wouldn't be a marriage. It would be like sharing digs with an Army P.T. instructor.'

'If it's the frustrated paternal instinct which is worrying him, dear,' Nikki remarked, 'she's certainly aggressively fertile.'

'But he used to be most particular over the girls he was seen with in public,' I said, still puzzled. 'Almost as much as his waistcoats. I suppose he must develop some sort of blind spot when he starts looking for one for keeps, like Henry the Eighth.'

'Or perhaps he's just fond of massage,' suggested Nikki.

'God knows what the woman's doing to his muscular system!' I exclaimed. 'For years it hasn't been subjected to any greater strain than raising pints of beer.'

But Grimsdyke seemed in great spirits when the next morning he telephoned our surgery.

'Isn't she wonderful?' he asked at once. 'Lulu I mean. I've never met a woman in my life with so much of the vital force they used to teach us about in biology. I'm delighted you approve of her, old lad.'

'Just one second,' I interrupted him, wondering how to break the news as tactfully as possible. 'It's not that I disapprove, Grim. But frankly I don't think she's quite your genetic type.'

'But you *did* approve,' he insisted. 'You said the weather was going to change.'

'I certainly did not,' I replied indignantly. 'I may have got a little confused over the whole damn silly business, but I never said anything like that.'

There was a pause.

'You're behaving pretty badly to an old friend, if I may say so.'

'I'm not behaving badly at all,' I returned hotly. 'It was a stupid idea in the first place.'

'What the devil do you mean by stupid? Ever since you got married you've been behaving as though you were suffering from premature middle age. There's no need to be superior about chaps showing a bit of enterprise.'

'I'm only being superior about chaps making bloody fools of themselves.'

'Anyway, it's too late now,' he said briefly. 'I'm flying to spend the Christmas holidays with her family in Helsinki.'

'You haven't proposed to her?' I asked in alarm.

'As it happens I haven't. And it isn't any affair of yours if I do. You've simply got no taste for women, Simon. How you managed to land such a nice one as Nikki has always been as much a mystery as why she ever accepted you anyway.'

'Now look here——'

'Being a gentleman, I do not wish to bandy a lady's name about on the telephone wires any further,' he said loftily. 'Good-bye. Oh, and Merry Christmas,' he added, ringing off.

I felt annoyed with myself. I should have foreseen that any disapproval of Lulu would be immediately consumed in the flames of his passion. I supposed it was an oversight that I shared with a good many fathers who'd made the fruitless journey to Gretna Green. But it was clear that I couldn't let him go ahead and marry the woman if there was any chance of preventing it.

'Why, she'd kill him in six months,' I said anxiously to Nikki that evening.

'She might turn out to be a very sweet and gentle wife, of course.'

I snorted. 'So might Brunhild, but I personally wouldn't care to take a risk on it. Anyway, Grimsdyke's a very delicate organism. He'd need as much care over breeding in captivity as the giant panda.'

We suggested several ways of spoiling his romance, until our discussion of Grimsdyke's sex-life was interrupted by a consequence of our own, as Dr Pheasant rattled up in her car.

'It won't be long now,' she said to me, coming downstairs afterwards. 'Give us a ring as soon as the balloon goes up, old thing. I need a bit of time to start the old bus sometimes in this weather.'

'But we'll get plenty of warning with the first one, surely?' I remembered all the hours spent drinking cups of tea in cold front parlours round St Swithin's.

She gave me a severe glance. 'Can't say. The process isn't run by clockwork, you know.'

'No, of course not,' I apologised.

'Look at that case in the paper this morning. The wife of this shipping millionaire fellow—what's her name . . .'

'Not Lady Corrington?'

'That's it. Went to Switzerland for her Christmas holidays, and had the little brat in a Geneva clinic a month premature.'

I started to laugh, but she went on, 'Then there's this actress woman you used to hear so much about, Monica Fairchild. I had a bit of a chin-wag at the Royal College the other day with your Turtle Supe—he's looking after

her, you know. And the fuss! Letters, phone calls, tele-
grams, almost every half-hour. And do you know what?
Everyone's made a mistake. She's having it a month late.'

'So she's really having one!' I exclaimed. 'I bet she
cracked the whip at her husband.' Dr Pheasant looked
puzzled, so I went on, 'I don't suppose Turtle happened
to say anything about Monica Fairchild's secretary, did
he?'

'As a matter of fact, her secretary turned up with a note
while we were there. Big fellow called Catchpole.'

'Not a woman?' I asked in surprise.

'Definitely a man,' said Ann Pheasant.

17

THE next afternoon I went down to St Swithin's for the last gastric clinic before Christmas. It was held for only a handful of patients, whose normal expressions of dyspeptic gloom were deepened by the prospect of facing the festivities on a glass of milk and a biscuit. I found the wards as usual heavily decorated with paper chains and seasonal frescoes made by the patients—Christmas in hospital being largely an extension of occupational therapy —and the corridors lined with advertisements for students' performances under such titles as *Physiotherapy Phollies*, *Babies in the Ward*, and *Jack and the Bedpan*. These entertainments were as rigidly traditional as the old miracle plays, and it now seemed many years since Grimsdyke, Tony Benskin, and myself had given almost the same productions with a firkin of beer on a stretcher and a couple of understudies to replace any actors who happened to fall before the curtain did. At the time we felt that the hospital had never enjoyed such a set of enterprising, good-mannered, and highly intelligent students as ourselves; and though the young men and women now rehearsing noisily in the clinical demonstration rooms off the main corridors undoubtedly thought the same, I suppose in our hearts we still believed it.

When the clinic was over, Dr Pennyworth asked the three of us back to his house for a glass of sherry. Dr Granley-Dowkins had to refuse because of an acute mania in Ealing, but Mr Cambridge and I drove to Queen Anne Street, where the senior physician lived in elegant bachelorhood with his collection of Bristol glass and a housekeeper resembling Mrs Squeers. He was a slight, bald, quiet man, with an old-fashioned Daimler, an old-fashioned chauffeur, and old-fashioned manners, who whispered his way round his patients and materialised at each bedside like a courteous ghost, and was probably the last physician in London to wear spats and write his prescriptions in Latin.

'Has Sir Lancelot gone back to Hereford?' Dr Pennyworth asked as we stood round the fire sipping sherry which, like himself, seemed paler and dryer than normal.

'He's still staying with me,' replied Mr Cambridge briefly.

'Is he?' Dr Pennyworth looked surprised. 'I haven't seen him much in the club recently.'

'I don't think he has much time to go to it. He's very occupied with the bicentenary, you know.'

'Isn't he going to his own home for Christmas?' I asked.

Mr Cambridge shook his head.

'Surely he won't wish to leave Lady Spratt all alone at this season?' remarked Dr Pennyworth.

'He isn't leaving her all alone,' said Mr Cambridge gloomily. 'She's going off on a cruise.'

'A very original idea for Lady Spratt,' Dr Pennyworth observed.

'It wasn't her idea, it was mine,' complained Mr Cambridge. 'I saw an advertisement. It was in the paper.

It struck me that he himself might like to get away for a few weeks into the sunshine. Very reasonable for a man of his age.'

'Very reasonable,' agreed Dr Pennyworth.

'So I suggested a cruise. But he simply turned it into an opportunity to stay a bit longer in London. Not of course that I'm anything but delighted to entertain him over Christmas. One would have been equally honoured to entertain Lister or Harvey. But . . . well, Christmas is supposed to be a sort of family occasion,' he went on morosely. 'And I was rather looking forward to spending it with my girls. I hardly get to know them these days, apart from the fortnight when we all play cricket together on the sands.'

Mr Cambridge sounded so miserable that I said, 'Look here—I've got a large house on my hands, and we could easily change our plans and have him to stay with us. Nikki's unlikely to go off before New Year's Day at the earliest. And after all, I have got some sort of family connexion with him.'

'It's very kind of you, Simon. Very kind of you indeed. As a matter of fact I've already suggested it,' Mr Cambridge confessed. 'But he won't go. Too much work, he says, for the bicentenary.'

'I really can't understand why he's taking such an enthusiastic interest in it,' frowned Dr Pennyworth.

Sir Lancelot certainly knew about the knighthood—he had known about everything at St Swithin's for the last forty years—but as he had literally cut his own way into the titled ranks many years before I suspected that he just wanted to dish Mr Cambridge's chances and pay out Mrs Cambridge for all those red-hot instruments.

'There was a painful scene, a most painful scene, the other night,' said Mr Cambridge, who after a second glass of sherry began to unbottle his troubles. 'I had to inform Mr McCurdie, the sculptor, that we had changed our minds about his statue. I asked him round to my house. He is a perfectly charming fellow,' he explained to me. 'And quite a gentleman. You wouldn't think he was an artist for one moment. But like all these people he is somewhat strong-minded.'

The surgeon paused.

'He arrived rather angry. He's a big man, you know, with a beard. In fact, he looks rather like Sir Lancelot when he was younger. He said some very unkind things. Very unkind indeed. He quite frightened my three girls. I must confess I got rather uneasy myself.'

'You explained he would receive financial compensation, of course?' asked Dr Pennyworth.

'Naturally. But that only made him grow rather contemptuous. I think I could have handled him in the end —after all, in our work we're especially trained to deal with violent and excitable people—but unfortunately Sir Lancelot heard the noise, and took issue.'

Seeming unable to bring himself to describe the evening further, Mr Cambridge drank another glass of sherry.

'Unfortunate, perhaps, that you didn't arrange for your guest to be out,' murmured Dr Pennyworth.

'That's the trouble. I'd expected Sir Lancelot to be at the meeting of the International Fraternity of Surgeons. But he didn't go on that particular night—that's one of those infuriating knacks of his, always being where you don't expect him. He simply came out of his sitting-room and started on Mr McCurdie. I've never seen him quite so angry before, except when a patient had the temerity to question his treatment. But I fear that for once Sir Lancelot met something like his match.'

'I don't think you can browbeat an artist,' reflected the physician.

'Particularly one who spends his life banging away at great hunks of rock,' I added.

'Sir Lancelot started by accusing Mr McCurdie of insulting the intelligence of the medical profession. Mr McCurdie replied he was beginning to suspect that was impossible. Sir Lancelot said that he'd seen better objects produced by a pottery class for criminal lunatics. Mr McCurdie replied that if he had the aesthetic appreciation of a Broadmoor warder he couldn't do anything about it. Sir Lancelot then shouted "You are being abominably rude!" And Mr McCurdie shouted back that he was being rude to uphold the principles of artistic freedom, while Sir Lancelot was being rude only because he couldn't help it.

'Sir Lancelot next called Mr McCurdie an overblown stonemason, and Mr McCurdie called Sir Lancelot something like a presumptuous tripe-slicer. It was terrible. They had quite lost control of themselves. Two of my daughters were in tears and the dog was barking. There they were, glaring at each other with their beards almost touching, in the middle of my hearthrug. For a moment I thought they were coming to blows. It would have been most undignified.'

'And Lancelot a member of the Parthenon,' murmured Dr Pennyworth.

'I hope it came all right in the end?' I asked nervously.

'My wife,' explained Mr Cambridge, 'jumped into the breach. She is rather adept at such situations. Perhaps you remember in Sir Lancelot's theatre, the day he had that terrible row with the anaesthetist? I'm afraid that Celia doesn't quite understand what a great man Sir Lancelot is. We have had one or two most unfortunate episodes in the house, particularly when he has commented on her cooking. On one occasion she put a red-hot vegetable dish into his hands, I suspect not entirely accidentally. But I think that evening she put both Sir Lancelot and the sculptor rather to shame. Mr McCurdie left shortly afterwards, threatening to send writs.'

'Then I expect you've heard the last of it,' said Dr Pennyworth hearteningly.

Mr Cambridge shook his head.

'The next morning,' he went on in a pathetic voice, 'Sir Lancelot announced he was instructing his solicitors to start proceedings against Mr McCurdie, for about a dozen things from breach of contract to common assault and battery. He can't bring himself to discuss anything else, and he's making all sorts of terrible threats. He's talking of briefing half a dozen famous counsel. No one can reason with him, or even get a word in edgeways.'

'I tried hard to dissuade him. I told him it would all be most frightfully expensive. And then——' Mr Cambridge swallowed. 'Then he explained it would all be paid for out of the Bicentenary Fund. That's the one all the hospital graduates subscribed to. I'm sure they don't want their money spent on litigation.'

'I certainly don't want my own thirty bob spent on it,' I told him warmly.

'My wife—I mean I—was particularly anxious to take charge of the bicentenary personally. And now Sir Lancelot's managed to scotch every single idea of my own, and is going to fill the place with foreign surgeons, six of whom are to be billeted in my house. Dear me, dear me! I don't know what I shall do. I really don't.'

Mr Cambridge abruptly collapsed in a chair and held his head in his hands.

'My dear fellow! Have another glass of sherry?' said Dr Pennyworth in alarm.

'If there's any way in which I can possibly help——'

Mr Cambridge didn't hear us.

'And that's not all,' he went on. He stared fixedly into the fireplace. 'Far from it. I don't mind Sir Lancelot spending an hour in the bathroom every morning. I don't mind him thumping about in his room half the night doing his Japanese exercises. Not a bit. Such things must be allowed a man of Sir Lancelot's standing. I don't mind him ordering all our meals, whatever the expense. I don't even jib at pig's trotters once a week, if he happens to be fond of them. I didn't even complain about his instructing my daughters in the facts of life. With coloured diagrams.'

He silently wiped his glasses.

'But the real trouble,' he declared quietly, 'is the television.'

'Ah yes,' I recalled. 'He has views——'

'I bought a television set a few months ago,' Mr Cambridge went on. 'I thought it might amuse the girls. I can't understand the programmes very well myself. Sir Lancelot noticed it, of course, as soon as he moved in. He was rather rude about it. He said it was more demoralising than honest debauchery out in the open. Why, from the way he carried on you'd have imagined that I'd opened a house of ill-repute.

'After that, of course, we never dared turn it on. The

girls were very upset. They seemed to have become very attached to some of the performers. Then one evening, as it was getting near Christmas, I took Celia and the girls to a musical comedy as a treat. As so often happens, as soon as the performance started I was called out to see a case. It didn't seem worth going back to the theatre, and I don't care much for that sort of thing anyway, so I went straight home. What do you think I found? Lancelot in the sitting-room, looking at the television.

' "Just doing some sociological research," he explained.

'He seemed a little put out, and not wishing to disturb him I said I'd sit in the dining-room.

' "Interesting study, the media of mass-hypnosis," he told me.

'I agreed with him, of course.

' "One must put oneself out to inspect such things from time to time," he said. He didn't refer to the incident again.'

'So after that you could turn your television on some-times?' I suggested.

'After that,' said Mr Cambridge solemnly, 'we could never turn the damn thing off. Sir Lancelot does socio-logical research every evening—right from the moment those peculiar young men appear and start talking about the weather. My wife has to get the evening meal early and when I'm late I have to eat mine in the kitchen. If anyone speaks or wants the light on there's hell to pay. Dear me, dear me! I really find some of the items difficult to sit through. But I have to watch the lot because he likes discussing everything with me afterwards. Then he has to have his eggs boiled for exactly two minutes, and a special kind of blacking for his shoes, and as he doesn't believe in laundries my wife has to starch his collars and press his suits. And then there's this fuss about no one opening his particular newspapers and—My God, is that the time? I shall be out in the kitchen again.'

Mr Cambridge sprang up, and snatching his hat without another word made for the door.

'Bertie is far from himself,' observed Dr Pennyworth.

'I feel rather responsible for it all,' I told him. 'If it hadn't been for this baby we're having, Sir Lancelot would never have come to London in the first place.'

We stood on the doorstep watching the surgeon disappear towards Cavendish Square, distractedly trying to remember where he had parked his car.

Dr Pennyworth shook his head. 'Perhaps it would have been as well if Granley-Dowkins had been able to come along this evening after all,' he remarked softly.

18

NIKKI and I spent Christmas within safe distance of base at her parents' house in Richmond, where for me the festivities were overshadowed less by my wife's condition, or the image of Sir Lancelot in a paper hat presiding over the Cambridge's table, than the bright new sports car my brother-in-law had bought himself. I needed to invoke powerfully the spirit of the season to prevent myself dwelling on the injustice of feckless young men roaring about the countryside in fast cars when they should instead be having wives and babies.

It was clear that by the time I could afford a sports car myself my reflexes would have become too slow to risk driving it, and I was resigned to the small old saloon in which we drove home late on Boxing Day, ready for the casualties of Christmas at the next morning's surgery. As soon as we got in I pottered round our cold unfriendly rooms like a good householder, and returning to the sitting-room was surprised to find Nikki beside the empty fireplace reading a book.

'That must be pretty interesting,' I remarked. 'You haven't even taken your coat off.'

She held up the title. I read *The Elements of Practical Midwifery*.

'I think I've started,' she announced.

'No! Not already?'

'I'm absolutely certain. I've got a definite backache. It began just as we were driving through London.'

'That's certainly the first sign,' I agreed.

'It's starting to come and go, too.'

I paused, considering the symptoms.

'Let's have a look at the book again,' I said.

After half an hour of diagnostic dithering which would have made any of our own patients promptly telephone another adviser, we concluded that Nikki was in fact experiencing the onset of the first stage of labour.

'Right,' I said, getting up. 'I'll telephone Ann Pheasant.'

'And what shall *I* do?' Nikki asked.

I scratched my head. I couldn't remember being consulted at such an early period.

'Go to bed, I suppose.'

'No I'm not. I'm going to clean out the kitchen,' she said firmly.

'Clean out the kitchen? Don't be ridiculous! Not now.'

'Yes I am. Otherwise I won't have a chance before your parents arrive and think I'm a messy housewife. Besides, domestic activity is traditional.'

Ann Pheasant wasn't at her surgery. There was no reply from her lodgings, and I was beginning to feel anxious when someone came on the line and told me to call the obstetrical department of the local Memorial Hospital.

'Hello, old thing,' she said, reaching the telephone after a delay which seemed several hours. 'What's up?'

'Nikki's gone into labour,' I explained quickly. 'I hope you're not in the middle of another case?'

'No, I'm in the middle of a hospital party.' From her tone I gathered she was rather enjoying herself. 'You're quite sure?'

'Yes, of course I'm sure. Perfectly.'

'Oh, very well. I'll be along as soon as I can decently detach myself. Keep her quiet and comfortable.'

I found Nikki on her hands and knees with a bucket, scrubbing the kitchen floor.

'Darling,' I protested. 'I'm perfectly sure you shouldn't be doing that.'

She laughed. 'Don't look so alarmed, Simon. Anyone would think you were about to have it instead of me.'

'I *am* rather alarmed,' I confessed. 'Even though I must have told hundreds of husbands it's a perfectly natural process.'

'But there's hours to go before anything dramatic happens. Though perhaps you'd better ring up our parents and tell them the overture has started. Besides, it'll give you something to do,' she added, taking charge of my treatment.

I was surprised to find myself, despite nine months' warning and my professional education, in a peculiarly agitated state. It didn't seem possible that in a few hours time I should be holding my own offspring and watching it being sick down my tie. I pottered round the house, moving things about. I tried to read a magazine, but it was as useless as trying to read one in a dentist's waiting-room. Nikki meanwhile went on scrubbing the kitchen.

F

'Perhaps I had better go upstairs,' she announced, appearing some time later drying her hands on a dish-cloth.

'How's the backache?'

'Worse.'

'Still intermittent?'

She nodded.

'Then perhaps you'd better.'

I stayed in the cold sitting-room. I paced about. I seemed to get through a lot of matches lighting my pipe.

The doorbell rang.

'Thank God!' I cried.

I threw open the front door, and was face to face with Grimsdyke.

'What the devil are you doing here?' I demanded, with unreasonable ferocity.

But instead of seeming put out, he flung out his hand.

'I agree, old lad. Exactly the sort of greeting I deserve.'

'But what on earth——'

'After the way I spoke to you on the phone, you really ought to kick me all round your crazy paving. I was an idiot, a fool and an ungrateful cad. Since then,' he said sombrely, 'I have been both sorry and humbled.'

'Oh, damn what you said on the phone! I was expecting our doctor. Nikki's in labour.'

'Good Lord, is she? But surely all that's next week?'

'You know as well as I do that a week one way or another——'

'Yes, yes, old lad. And at such a time even I can feel that I'm definitely a bit superfluous. I'll come back in a couple of days when all the smoke's died down.'

'No, come on in,' I said, changing my mind. 'As a matter of fact, I'd rather like someone to hold my hand. It's all a bit nerve-racking. That's why I was so short just now. Sorry.'

'Don't mention it. If you really want me to stay, offering my company at such a time is not only a pleasure but a duty. I'm staying in Hampden Cross a few days, by the way. At the Hat and Feathers, of course—I knew you wouldn't want me mucking about here.'

'But what's the matter with your flat?'

He looked a little uncomfortable.

'Fact is, I've rather got to make myself scarce from London for a week or two.'

'What, not again?'

But further enquiries were forestalled by the arrival of a midwife on a bicycle, followed much more noisily a few moments later by Ann Pheasant's car.

'Sorry I'm a bit late, old thing,' the obstetrician greeted me. 'The old bus took a bit of starting. Fortunately one of the registrars got it going with a bottle of ether in the petrol tank. Heard a lot about you,' she said, as I introduced Grimsdyke. 'And how's the patient?'

'Sitting up in bed reading *Barchester Towers*.'

'Jolly sensible. It's as good a sedative as any in the pharmacopoeia.'

'Anything I can do?' I asked anxiously, as she brought her bag inside.

'Nothing, except forget you're a doctor.'

I left Ann with Nikki upstairs. Retiring to the sitting-room, I fetched a bottle of whisky I'd hidden in one of the fretwork bookcases.

'How's Lulu,' I asked Grimsdyke, mainly to keep my thoughts off the proceedings.

I might have mentioned one of his distant relatives.

'Lulu? All right I suppose.'

'You mean,' I asked, my hopes rising, 'that she's turned you down?'

'Turned me down? No, nobody's turned me down.' He looked shocked at the idea. 'I've just had a very interesting time with her people. If I don't see so much of her in the next few weeks it's only because old McGlew's shortly taking his aches and pains back to New York.'

'Come off it,' I said. 'Even I can diagnose that the fever of love has abated by several degrees.'

'Not exactly, old lad,' he told me, still sounding hurt. 'You wouldn't think that of me, surely? But—well, they say if you're going to marry someone the great thing is to have the same tastes all along the line, don't they?'

I poured a couple of stiff drinks.

'And where did yours and Lulu's diverge?'

'We had rather a disagreement over this beastly bath business.'

'Bath business? But you have quite a lot of baths. When we shared a flat you were always hogging all the hot water.'

'Not that sort of bath. Personally I don't think I could start the day without half an hour in the warm water with a packet of cigarettes and the crossword. But there's a limit to everything. Having spent her life periodically charging naked through Scandinavian pine-forests, Lulu is a great one for the *sauna*.'

'That's a kind of fish they serve in Swedish restaurants, isn't it?'

'It certainly is not. It's a sort of supercharged Turkish bath, which is all the rage in Finland and such arctic places. Anyway,' he interrupted himself. 'You won't want to hear all about it just now.'

'Yes, I do. It'll keep my mind distracted, like the *Arabian Nights*.'

'Well, we arrived at Helsinki airport—jolly expensive trip it was, now you come to think of it—to be greeted warmly by Lulu's fond family.'

'The old Count?'

'Actually, he's a bank manager. I must say I rather expected chaps in boots dancing all over the place to the balalaika, but it's all very civilised. Trams, you know. We had quite a jolly party, drinking schnapps and eating cold fish sandwiches. Then Lulu insisted the two of us went off to the local *sauna*.

'Like a fool,' Grimsdyke went on sombrely, 'I agreed. Fact is, I'd heard vaguely it was a sort of communal bath, like the ones you have after playing rugger. But with mixed bathing allowed. I thought it might be rather agreeable to see Lulu strolling about without her vest on, not to mention lots of other beautiful blondes. Don't misunderstand me,' he added quickly. 'It's all done in a very hearty spirit and above board. Nothing sordid, just sunlight and fresh air to the pores.'

'Of course,' I said.

I looked at my watch. Ann Pheasant seemed already to have been upstairs a terrifyingly long time.

'That was my first mistake,' said Grimsdyke disconsolately. 'We arrived at this place, which looked very seasonable in the snow among the Christmas trees, but at the front door Lulu promptly bade me good-bye. The communal idea was just another of those fine old national customs that have died out, like dancing round the maypole. Ladies' night was on Thursdays.

'I went inside and found myself in a place like the locker room of some posh golf club, with another lot of chaps. I was just wondering if I might get out of it all by pretending to make a phone call, when I was unfortunately befriended by a native. A fellow with a beard, who looked like Ibsen pondering over some particularly gloomy plot.

' "Here is the undressing," explained the Ibsen chap.

' "Right-ho," I said, as bravely as anyone. But I'd only undone my cuff-links when a homely-looking old dear in a white dress came in and started messing about with a pile of towels.

' "But what about her?" I asked.

' "What about her?" asked the chap, taking off his trousers.

'An Englishman,' continued Grimsdyke feelingly, 'has to kick over a ruddy great heap of inhibitions before he starts unclothing himself in front of casual females. But I couldn't let the old country down, could I? So I went ahead. But as a sort of compromise I kept my pipe in my mouth.

'I followed Ibsen into a narrow room with a wooden bench down each side,' he explained, sipping his whisky. 'It was just like those old French third-class carriages.

' "What happens here?" I asked.

' "Here we sweat," he said.

'And we did, too. It was like assisting at one of Sir

Lancelot's total pancreatectomies in the middle of Ascot week. The stuff poured off me. And all the while I couldn't help thinking of Lulu doing the same thing every Thursday. Rather tarnished the glamour a bit, if you follow me.'

There was a bump upstairs.

'Do you want me?' I shouted.

'Relax, old thing! Relax!' came Dr Pheasant's voice.

'Sorry,' I apologised to Grimsdyke, sitting down again. 'I'm a bit edgy.'

'Understandable,' he said, taking one of my cigarettes. 'And what happened after that?'

'By the time I was feeling totally dehydrated old Ibsen shepherded me into a tiled place like St Swithin's out-patients', where a lot of Scandinavian-looking coves were splashing about in showers. They all looked pretty gloomy about it, just like we do when we're enjoying our cricket. I splashed about too, congratulating myself on coming out uncoagulated, when Ibsen pushed me into another one of their ruddy ovens. I thought the first one was hot, but this was like taking a stroll through a blast-furnace. There was also a stove in the corner apparently made of disused paving-stones, which the devilish fellow started chucking buckets of water over. Phew! The steam pretty well stripped off your epidermis. Frankly, I thought I'd had it, and my charred remains would be shipped back to England, to the derision of the entire local populace. But the old boy seemed to enjoy it all no end, rubbing his great hairy chest and saying, "Very healthy, very healthy. No germs can live in the *sauna*. In the country many people are born in them."

'I asked how many people died in them,' Grimsdyke

added, 'but he just looked a bit cross and said, "Now, we shall have the wash."'

'In the room next door,' my friend went on, staring steadily into his whisky glass, 'were two tables with wooden headrests, like the ones we used to do our anatomy dissection on. And in the middle was another motherly old dear in a white dress, washing the customers.'

'Grim!' I cried in horror. 'You didn't——?'

'Well, I couldn't let the side down, could I? And I was damned if Lulu was going to hear I'd funked it. So I let myself be subjected to an indignity, old lad, that I haven't suffered since I was six. And the worst part was the washer-woman being the spit and image of the old duck who comes to scrub my flat floor. Have to sack her, of course, as soon as I get back.'

'What a soul-testing experience,' I murmured.

'Even that wasn't the end of it. Ibsen suggested we beat ourselves all over with birch twigs—just the thing for keeping out the cold in Finland, possibly, but it would look pretty nasty if ever it got on your psychological case-sheet, wouldn't it?'

' "Then we shall enjoy instead the ice-cold plunge," said Ibsen, pointing to a lake outside where some chaps had broken the ice. But—thank God!—I can't swim. I never learnt somehow. It always looked too wet and uncomfortable to try. I told him all I wanted was my trousers back.'

'Anyway, it's all supposed to be very good for your adrenal glands,' I consoled him. 'Or so I read somewhere. Makes them excrete the ketosteroids.'

'My dear old lad, my adrenal glands felt like a couple of squeezed oranges. I suppose that's why I found Lulu

waiting rather expectantly—after a *sauna* a chap's supposed to behave like a mixture of Sandow the Strong Man,
Falstaff, and Casanova. But whether I've got the wrong
sort of adrenals or the wrong sort of upbringing, all I felt
was terribly ill. And the point is this—there's one of these
beastly places in London. It's up in Cricklewood, near
the crematorium. Lulu takes her sponge-bag there every
Friday night, and she expects me to go through the fiery
furnace once a week for the rest of my life just to keep my
endocrine system in trim for her. Personally, I think I'd
be dead in a couple of years from chronic heat-stroke.
Also, you keep seeing everyone's operation scars, and it's
damned disquieting being faced with the gravestones of
cholecystectomies and appendicectomies at every turn. The
only good thing I can see in the whole performance is
making Finnish surgeons a bit more fussy about their
incisions, instead of going out for a cup of tea and leaving
the sewing-up to the houseman.'

Grimsdyke fell into a thoughtful silence.

'The end of Lulu?' I asked quietly.

He hesitated. 'Rather unfortunately, old lad—that is,
approaching her with a slightly different end in view than
with the usual hotsie—I rather led her to understand——'

'You proposed?' I exclaimed. 'Then you *are* in trouble.'

'And of course, there's the other two girls I told you
about——'

'You didn't propose to those, too, you idiot?'

'I didn't actually *propose* to any of them,' he protested.
'The conversation somehow just drifted that way. Why,
it's just as easy to propose to a woman as to walk under
a bus! God knows how I can get out of it. I don't suppose
they'll land me in the Law Courts, but it could be dashed

awkward. Come to think of it,' he added, 'I don't believe I can stand the sight of all three of them. So what on earth am I going to do?'

'There's only one cure,' I said, after a minute's reflection. 'Get yourself married to another one.'

'What other one?' snorted Grimsdyke.

Prescribing for my friend's social ills was curtailed by the sound of the bedroom door shutting and the appearance of Dr Pheasant. Coming downstairs with her was Nikki.

'Nothing doing,' said Ann Pheasant briskly.

'Oh, no!'

Nikki looked apologetic. 'We made a mis-diagnosis.'

'False labour,' announced Ann. 'Very common in midwives, doctors, and nervous patients.'

'I'm terribly sorry, Ann,' Nikki said.

'How damn stupid of us!' I said. I myself felt far more foolish than contrite. 'But it did all seem to fit in so neatly with the book.'

'First rule of medicine—never go by the book.' The obstetrician looked at her hefty wrist watch. 'The party will probably be over by now. Pity.'

Ann Pheasant, the midwife, and Grimsdyke then tactfully left. I fell despondently into a chair.

'Now I know how a chap feels when he's got all ready for a parachute jump and they tell him it's his turn next week.'

'And I,' said Nikki, 'feel that I am going to remain exactly like this for the rest of my born days.'

'Cheer up, darling,' I consoled her wearily. 'It can't be more than another week or so at the most. Then you'll be quite missing your lump.'

'We mustn't bother Ann with any more false starts, at any rate.'

'I hope not, for your sake.'

'And for yours, dear. You've made quite a hole in that whisky.'

19

For the next week I treated Nikki with the delicacy of an unexploded bomb. Every time she stirred in her chair I asked hopefully if she had backache, and every time she woke me by turning over in bed I found myself reaching for the telephone.

My wife's precarious condition made any social plans impossible, though Grimsdyke paid a charitable call every evening, generally at the hour when he judged that I might be having a drink.

'The old uncle's asked me if I'd like to fill in my time by giving a hand with the practice while I'm here,' he mentioned one evening, as we passed through the midwinter doldrums between Christmas and New Year. 'I hardly had the heart to refuse the dear old fellow, he seemed so decently hesitant about suggesting it. But my literary work, old lad, comes first. These days I've hardly time to leave my bedroom at the Hat and Feathers for a quick one.'

'What, more jolly articles for the *Daily Hypochondriac*?'

'I've got a better idea than that,' he told me proudly. 'I'm writing a book. I got the idea when I drifted into your local newsagent's the other day to see when the next edition of Ruff's *Guide to the Turf* was coming out. They'd got rows of novels in there with chaps on the cover operating in their stethoscopes. It suddenly struck me how dearly the general public loves tales of gore among the gallipots—after all, you've only got to look at the speed they gather round a really satisfactory accident. And it should be pretty easy to write something sensational about hospitals, life and death being their stock-in-trade.'

'What's your book about?'

'Oh, a chap and a girl and another chap,' he said vaguely. 'But at least it'll occupy my exile. God knows how I'm ever going to face that Lulu woman again—did you spot the size of her hands?'

We again discussed Grimsdyke's emotional enmeshment, but I could think of no way to untangle him before he left, promising to return the following night to see in the New Year with me—Nikki having prescribed herself an early bed and a glass of milk.

As the practice was slack at the time I had the last afternoon of the old year to potter at home among the nappies and feeding-bottles, hoping they wouldn't disgrace the fearsomely experienced nurse I had engaged once the baby was delivered. Grimsdyke had bought a celluloid duck for the coming infant, and I was enjoying playing with this in the plastic baby's bath when I was interrupted by a ring at the doorbell. I thought this might be Ann Pheasant coming to seek news, and as Nikki had her feet up in the bedroom I went down to open the door.

I found on the mat a pleasant-looking dark-haired girl, grasping a large brass telescope.

'Dr Farquarson?' she asked.

'I'm afraid not. I'm his partner, Dr Sparrow.'

'So *you're* Dr Sparrow,' she smiled. 'I've heard a lot about you.'

'If there's anything I can do——?'

'It's a terribly silly business, really,' the girl apologised. 'But this object'—she held out the telescope—'has been on my conscience for months. There's a Dr Farquarson's name and address engraved on it, and as I was going through Hampden Cross in the car I thought I'd better return it. I suppose your receptionist sent me down here because he was out.'

'That's certainly his old telescope,' I agreed. 'He likes to look at the stars and so on with it. But how on earth did you manage to come across it?'

'My name's Zoë Mitchel, by the way——'

'Of course!' I exclaimed. 'Dr Grimsdyke—you found it on the boat?'

'Well . . . he presented me with it, as a matter of fact.' She laughed. 'Oh, there's quite a story.'

'Yes, I've heard it,' I said, smiling too.

'I hope Dr Grimsdyke wasn't too upset?'

'I think he was, rather. He came and stayed with us afterwards.'

She suddenly looked concerned. 'Did he think I'd treated him rather badly? But it *was* a bit of a shock. I'd never been proposed to in my life before. And coming like that—right in the middle of the games room.'

'Just one second,' I said quickly. 'Do you mean that *he*—my friend Grimsdyke—actually proposed to *you*?'

Zoë appeared flustered. 'But I thought you told

me you knew all about it. I wouldn't have dreamed otherwise——'

We were interrupted by a cry of, 'Any sign of the first triplet?' as Grimsdyke came gaily down the path.

'Good gracious, it's Gaston!' she exclaimed. 'Fancy running into you.'

I had always admired Grimsdyke's poise, which I had watched him maintain even in such testing circumstances as having his diagnosis questioned by Sir Lancelot Spratt. But now he stopped dead and seemed to droop all over, like a snowman in a burst of winter sunshine.

'Oh, hello Zoë,' he mumbled, after some time.

He stood slowly massaging the gastrocnemius muscle of his left calf with his right toe-cap.

'And how are you?' he managed to ask.

'I'm very well, thank you,' said Zoë quietly. 'And you?'

'Me? I'm very well, too. Thank you.'

'Good,' said Zoë.

There was a pause. A boy went past whistling on a bicycle, sounding like an express roaring through the station.

'Ankle all right now?' asked Grimsdyke.

'Perfectly all right, thank you,' said Zoë.

'Good,' said Grimsdyke.

There was another silence. As the conversation seemed to be getting neither of them anywhere, and I was also feeling chilly standing on the doorstep, I suggested, 'Perhaps you'd like to come in for a cup of tea, Miss Mitchel?'

'That's very kind of you, Dr Sparrow,' she said, both seeming relieved by my intervention.

'But I really ought to be getting on to London, as it's starting to get so misty.'

'It's generally only local.'

I became aware of Grimsdyke making rasping noises with his larynx, which I interpreted as an invitation to Zoë to take a spot of dinner.

She bit her lip. 'I don't think I possibly can,' she said. But after a moment that she could conceal from neither of us contained concentrated cerebration, she added, 'If you're quite sure the fog's only local . . . and if you don't mind if I do leave rather early——'

Suddenly looking more cheerful, Grimsdyke suggested showing her round the Abbey, a building I knew that he hadn't yet entered. After a little more disjointed conversation, they went off together in Zoë's car, leaving me holding the telescope.

'What on earth do you make of it all?' I exclaimed to Nikki, telling her the story. 'Old Grimsdyke's a deeper fish than even I imagined. From the look on his face there wasn't the slightest doubt the girl's telling the truth.'

'And is she really the horror he made out?'

'That's another mystery about it. She doesn't exactly look like an Italian film-star, but she's quite pretty and strikes me as a very decent sort. In fact, if he really wants to get married she'd be a far better proposition than all those others.'

Nikki frowned. 'Do you suppose,' she asked, 'that Grimsdyke is really just a little bit insane?'

'Oh, mad as a hatter, darling. Has been for years. Backache?' I demanded suddenly.

'Indigestion,' said Nikki.

I wondered what other plausible story my friend would

appear with later that evening, when Nikki went to bed leaving me with an article on gastroenterology in the *British Medical Journal*, which soon put me into a gentle doze at the fireside. The doorbell woke me with a start, and I noticed that it was already near eleven.

'I want to unburden my soul,' said Grimsdyke immediately, entering with swirls of fog.

'That soul of yours is getting a bit overloaded, isn't it?'

But he threw himself into a chair so despondently I immediately felt sorry for him.

'Anyway, Grim,' I added, 'after all we've been through together, I'm afraid you can always rely on me to give you advice.'

'All I told you about that boat,' he admitted at once, 'was pure ruddy rationalisation, like the psychiatrists keep talking about. You know, the same as when you want to buy a new car and kid yourself you'll save on train fares. The odd business is, you actually do believe it at the time. Stupid thing, the human mind, isn't it?'

'I'm sure no philosopher would disagree with you.'

'As far as I'm concerned, Zoë's the fairest blossom on the evolutionary tree,' he confessed simply. 'I wanted to marry her, old lad. So I asked her when the opportunity arose, which was during ping-pong. She mumbled something rather confused about thinking it over. Then, of course, I got cold feet.'

He paused to reach for my cigarettes.

'I suppose I'm a sort of Dr Jekyll and Dr Hyde. On one hand, I saw myself cosy with Zoë in a suburban semi-det. with all the buttons on my shirts. On the other, I was ploughing through stacks of dirty nappies to clip my eldest on the earhole for emptying my only bottle of beer over the other five. I know it's time I had a steady job and a smile from the bank manager, but it's dashed difficult to come to the point. Hence my recent erratic behaviour.'

'I should chose the semi-det. and nappies,' I told him. 'Most people do in the end.'

'Did I tell you old McGlew's offered me a decent job overseas? But there again, after my Poparapetyl experiences I'm certainly not going without a wife to keep me on the rails and apply the brakes as required.'

'And Zoë——?' I asked.

'Won't have me.'

He stared gloomily at his feet.

'Funny thing, it never occurred to me before that any girl wouldn't. We broached the subject again tonight— we could hardly help it, could we?—and all we agreed was never to establish contact again. I wouldn't even know where to find her, except she lives somewhere in Yorkshire. It would be the biggest ruddy county of the lot,' he added miserably.

'There are other girls, Grim,' I said, trying to cheer him up. 'Apart from Scandinavian masseuses.'

'But there aren't! Fact is, old lad,' he explained, as though confessing some shameful felony. 'I love her.'

Nikki called from upstairs.

'She forgot her New Year's glass of milk,' I told him. 'Just a minute while I fetch it from the kitchen.'

But when I reached the bedroom one glance at my wife's face was enough.

'Good God!' I exclaimed. 'How long——?'

'All afternoon . . .'

She paused, gripping my hand tightly. It was a moment before she could go on. 'I felt such a fool getting Ann the last time, I really wanted to make sure——'

'Let me have a look at your tummy,' I said, deciding it was the moment for professional briskness.

'Regular and strong contractions,' I agreed, replacing the bedclothes. 'Now don't worry, darling—I'll ring Ann this very second, and tell her to hurry.'

Grimsdyke jumped to his feet as I rushed downstairs. 'What's up?'

'Nikki. In the second stage.'

'Good God! Shall I clear off?'

'No, don't. You may be useful.'

This time Ann Pheasant was at a New Year's party in the midwives' hostel.

'You're quite sure, old thing?'

'Sure? Of course I'm sure. She's terribly far gone.'

'Oh, all right. Give her some pethidine and I'll bring the midwife with me. I haven't time to see the New Year in, I suppose?'

'You certainly haven't!'

I boiled up a syringe in a saucepan and gave Nikki a hundred milligrams of pethidine. Afterwards I divided my time between holding her hand and getting things ready for Ann Pheasant. Grimsdyke meanwhile sat downstairs, looking more frightened than either of us.

'Hasn't the damn woman come yet?' I demanded, bursting again into the sitting-room.

'Only twenty minutes since you rang her, old lad,' murmured Grimsdyke uncomfortably. 'Nikki all right?'

'A bit too all right.'

But after forty minutes had passed even Grimsdyke couldn't try to reassure me. When the telephone rang we both jumped like shot rabbits.

'Hello?'

'Had a bit of trouble starting the car, old thing,' said Ann calmly. 'But it's all right. I've warmed up the plugs in the autoclave.'

'For God's sake do hurry,' I implored her. 'Things are really going on fast.'

'Don't look so worried, old lad,' said Grimsdyke, trying to raise a smile as I put down the telephone. 'After all, there are three doctors in the house. But why not ring up the old uncle? As a sort of insurance policy, in case this Pheasant woman blows a gasket.'

'What a good idea!' I exclaimed, clasping him gratefully.

I rang the flat over our surgery, but the call was taken by a sleepy receptionist.

'What's the trouble now?' asked Grimsdyke, noticing my face.

'He's out,' I explained briefly. 'On a maternity case.'

We passed another fifteen minutes. Nikki was now trying to reassure me as much as I tried to reassure her. Grimsdyke looked like someone invited to a party which turns out much rowdier than he expected.

The telephone rang again. Ann Pheasant was lost in the fog.

'That's the trouble with female doctors!' I exploded unfairly. 'They always let you down in a crisis.'

I gave our obstetrician another ten minutes, then I made my decision.

'Yes, it is a bit hot in here, old lad,' said Grimsdyke, watching as I took my jacket off.

'Not as hot as it's going to be for all of us in a minute. I'm going to do the delivery myself.'

His eyebrows shot up.

'I suppose it's our own fault for putting the wind up Ann Pheasant last time,' I said. I felt surprisingly calm once I knew what I had to face. 'Could you give me a hand?'

Grimsdyke didn't hesitate. 'Of course, Simon. For all our fooling about over the years, we've never let the old profession down over a job of work, have we?'

'I'll boil up some scissors and needles in the kitchen,' I told him. 'You go and collect the trilene inhaler from the boot of the car.'

But I had hardly left the sitting-room when Grimsdyke appeared from the garage with a shout of, 'It's all right, old lad! Panic over. She's here. Look—two ruddy great headlights in the fog.'

'Thank God!' I cried.

I ran to the front door. A figure came stamping through the darkness.

'I have just undergone the most insulting experience of my life,' declared Sir Lancelot Spratt.

'That preposterous woman!' he continued, coming straight inside. 'How the devil Cambridge ever married her is totally beyond me. She threw me out. Me! After I had been putting up with their extremely indifferent hospitality, not to mention taking considerable pains to be of no trouble to anyone, she had the effrontery to hurl ill-mannered abuse at my head and order me out of the house. Can you imagine such behaviour among civilised human beings? And on such a trivial excuse! Just because

I wanted to see something on channel nine, when she for some reason insisted on watching some rubbish on channel one——'

'For God's sake shut up!' I snapped.

My godfather stared at me.

'Have you taken leave of your senses too, boy?' he roared.

'I'm sorry,' I said shortly. I told him the situation in the house.

Sir Lancelot immediately became grave. He looked round like a new commander in a demoralised garrison.

'And if your obstetrician remains lost,' he asked, stroking his beard, 'who, pray, will do the delivery?'

'I will.'

'You will not. For a doctor to take clinical responsibility for his wife in childbed is wholly unfair to all three participants. Where is the patient?'

'The room at the top of the stairs.'

'Right. It is perhaps fortunate that I have always regarded myself as a general surgeon in the widest sense. You are unaware that I delivered a woman in a somewhat similar situation while holidaying in Ireland last year? I fear,' he continued with some satisfaction, 'it might be beyond the abilities of some of my younger colleagues who now charge more and more for treating less and less. I am glad to see you have the latest automatic inhaler there,' he continued, catching sight of my friend.

'You will take charge of it, Dr Grimsdyke. The apparatus is claimed by its designers to be foolproof, and now we shall have a chance to find out. Sparrow, you will stay out of everybody's way. Fetch me a surgical mask, some hot water, and a clean hand towel.'

With a step that bore a lifetime's experience of life and death, of men and women, and of the greatest joys and tragedies human beings can experience, Sir Lancelot Spratt went calmly upstairs.

20

I HAD prepared myself to experience all manner of noble feelings when I first looked at my son. But as I rushed upstairs after Grimsdyke's shout, 'Right-ho, Simon, you can order a set of trains—it's a boy!' all I could think as I inspected the pink and noisy lump was, 'Good Lord! Did I do that?'

The rest of the night was rather confused. Ann Pheasant arrived shortly after the baby (as I am sure all five of us had more than once as midwifery students), and seeming demoralised by the presence of Sir Lancelot made a few remarks about abnormally rapid labours and withdrew. Nikki sat serenely in bed, holding her baby and drinking the traditional cup of tea. My godfather looked highly pleased with himself, and even slapped Grimsdyke on the back. No one took much notice of me.

In an hour or two the nurse appeared and firmly took possession of the infant, and when I woke up after a doze on the sofa I found Grimsdyke frying bacon and eggs.

'I particularly want to be back for lunch at St Swithin's to-day,' explained Sir Lancelot, who was breakfasting in the kitchen. He seemed to smile at some inward joke. 'I intended only to sponge on you for a bed, even though it was that infernal canvas contraption. I might say that now I feel I've earned it.'

'You certainly have, sir.'

'I'll stay at the club for a while,' he told me, 'and then go back for a bit of rest to Hereford. I think I can leave the bicentenary to Cambridge, now I've put him on the right path. But first I would like a word with you and your wife, Sparrow. And the baby, too, if you like. After all, it concerns him.'

Nikki had just finished the early feed when Sir Lancelot and I appeared in the bedroom.

'I expect you know what I've got to say,' he began, after tickling young Lancelot's nose. 'Despite my some-what disillusioning experience when last in this house, I think, Sparrow, that you have somewhat surprisingly turned into a reasonable member of society. That the metamorphosis is entirely due to your charming wife I have no doubt whatever.'

Nikki smiled.

'And so my offer of financial assistance—not to you, but to the little brat who is at this moment interrupting me—still stands.'

I hesitated. Then I said, 'It's very kind of you, sir. We—we greatly appreciate it. But—if you don't mind—we'd rather just stand on our own six feet.'

Sir Lancelot said nothing. I wondered if I had detonated a delayed explosion.

'You are quite right,' he declared quietly after some moments. 'I think that I should have made precisely the same reply in similar circumstances. But I nevertheless

ask you to accept. It is you who are doing the kindness,
not me.'

My godfather got up and walked slowly about the room,
his hands clasped behind his tail coat.

'We all grow old,' he said. 'It is only physiological. The
dermis loses its elasticity and wrinkles. The *arcus senilis*
holds the iris in its embrace. The bones grow brittle, the
joints arthritic. Our temperatures fall, our metabolism
slows. But worst of all is a chilling of the spirit.'

He paused, with a look of humility I had seen before
only when he referred in lectures to famous professional
forbears.

'I've had a good life. But I suppose all I've really got to
show for it is a row of bottles in the St Swithin's pathology
museum. Oh, I know I've made a good many people more
comfortable. I've prolonged for a while a good many lives.
I might even have saved one or two. But a surgeon's on
earth to do surgery like a shoemaker's on earth to make
shoes. And neither has the right to get sentimental about
it.

'That is not to say I'm belittling the profession that all
three of us are privileged to belong to. I'm not. No man
or woman can do better than apply his life to maintaining
the health of his fellow creatures. Without health this
world seems to contain no comfort, and the next no
kindliness. And our reward is in the mind—a mind trained
to strip the pretences and prejudices that men cover
themselves with like their clothes. I believe it is only we
who discover what is basically good or bad underneath.
I should have hated to have lived without experiencing
that.'

He stood stroking his beard for some seconds. His

namesake stopped crying, yawned widely, and went to sleep.

'If I had children of my own, I should hope that one at least followed me to St Swithin's. You yourselves cannot realise at this moment what comfort that would be to me—to know that I had a personal interest in someone walking the same path not only of myself, but of Pasteur, John Hunter, or Horder. It is highly unlikely that I shall be in existence when this young man might decide to take up medicine. But it would be enough for me to feel that I was going to be of some help to him if he should.'

Sir Lancelot paused.

'I'm talking a lot,' he said briskly. 'I thought I wouldn't have to bare me soul like this, Sparrow. I imagined it would have been perfectly easy to have bullied you into it.'

'Of course, we accept, gratefully,' said Nikki. 'Don't we, Simon?'

'Then I'm delighted,' was all Sir Lancelot said.

'I was afraid before,' Nikki went on frankly, 'that you would terrorise us about how to bring him up.'

'Good God!' exclaimed Sir Lancelot. 'Me? Why, I'm scared stiff of children.'

Shortly afterwards my godfather left for London. 'I'll come back and see you one of these days,' he announced, as I bade him farewell at the door. 'Meanwhile,' he added, catching sight of an object on the hall table, 'I hope my wedding present will prove useful.'

'By the way, sir,' I asked, emboldened by our new relationship. 'What exactly is it?'

'My dear chap, I haven't the slightest idea. I picked it

up at an auction and have been trying to get rid of it for years.'

The fog had disappeared with the other trials of the night, and in crisp sunshine I picked up the papers and letters left unnoticed on the doormat. Then the telephone rang.

'It's for you,' I called to Grimsdyke. 'It's Zoë from London.'

'She wants me to take her out to lunch,' he exclaimed in delight, after a brief and almost whispered conversation. 'She actually wants me to buy her food. She rang up specially to find me. Do you realise what it means, Simon? Do you understand? She doesn't think I'm an uncouth great baboon after all. She agrees to be seen in public in my company. She actually wants to put up with my footling conversation. She's prepared to look at my vacuous great face. She's——'

'Take it easy, Grim,' I said, smiling. 'There's a long way to go between taking a girl out to lunch and leading her down the aisle.'

'But the Grimsdykes old lad,' he explained proudly, 'are fast and efficient workers, once they get their teeth into a job. Bet you a quid in another couple of years we'll be pushing our prams out together?'

I laughed.

'Done!'

'Just you wait and see. Must rush off now if I want to tidy up a bit in Town. Lots of love to mother and child. And thanks for the excitement.'

As he grabbed his corduroy cap and hurried down the path I absently looked at my letters. The first had an Australian stamp on it. I ripped open the envelope.

'*Sydney, N.S.W.*' it began simply.

'*Dear Doctor,*

Don't I turn up in the most peculiar places? I am living with Harold again and we are terribly happy. That nasty bit of baggage has gone off with a sheep farmer. I could have told him so. Harold was very, very naughty in England, and I'm going to see he works hard and pays every penny back in Hampden Cross. But with you he really could have got into awful trouble. It was all that baggage's fault. Harold is so sweet and simple he is easily led astray. That's why I'm insisting he makes it up to you first, with a big whack over as conscience money. I'm not putting our address, so you can't try and return it. Didn't I tell you I'm having a baby in July? Isn't it thrilling? No of course I didn't, I couldn't have been having it then, could I?

Love,
Diane Marston

Pinned to the letter was a cheque for five hundred pounds.

'The sports car!' I cried at once, any thought of providing for my new family basely obliterated. I was about to run upstairs to tell Nikki, when I found myself face to face with Sir Lancelot Spratt on the front page of the morning paper.

'But what on earth's the old boy been up to——'

Then I saw a headline saying NEW YEAR'S HONOURS LIST. Half-way down the column it announced simply—

BARONY FOR DOCTOR

Sir Lancelot Blyth Spratt, surgeon at St Swithin's Hospital, London, becomes a Baron for services rendered to international co-operation in medicine.

'Lord Spratt!' I gasped.

I stood still, letting the paper drop to the ground.

'So *that's* why the old boy has made such a fuss about the bicentenary. Poor old Cambridge—I only hope he wangles a knighthood for him one day. And by George,' I added, recovering from the shock, 'aren't those noble rafters going to ring at Westminster!'

After Nikki and I had laughed over the news I was allowed by the nurse the privilege of holding my son. It was almost impossible to believe that he too might one day go to St Swithin's, to sit in the same lecture benches, listen with the same inattention, react to the starkness of medical education with the same high spirits, play the same games, drink in the same pubs, fumble his way round the same wards, and flirt with much the same sort of nurses. Like Sir Lancelot and myself, he would become part of St Swithin's. But, more important, St Swithin's would always be part of us.